A Gift for

Elizabeth

by

Jann Rowland

One Good Sonnet Publishing
Publishers of Fine Romance
and Fantasy Fiction

By Jann Rowland

Published by One Good Sonnet Publishing:

PRIDE AND PREJUDICE VARIATIONS

Acting on Faith
A Life from the Ashes (Sequel to Acting on Faith)
Open Your Eyes
Implacable Resentment
An Unlikely Friendship
Bound by Love
Cassandra
Obsession
Shadows Over Longbourn
The Mistress of Longbourn
My Brother's Keeper
Coincidence
The Angel of Longbourn
Chaos Comes to Kent
In the Wilds of Derbyshire
The Companion
Out of Obscurity
What Comes Between Cousins
A Tale of Two Courtships
Murder at Netherfield
Whispers of the Heart
A Gift for Elizabeth

COURAGE ALWAYS RISES: THE BENNET SAGA

The Heir's Disgrace

Co-Authored with Lelia Eye

WAITING FOR AN ECHO

Waiting for an Echo Volume One: Words in the Darkness
Waiting for an Echo Volume Two: Echoes at Dawn

A Summer in Brighton
A Bevy of Suitors
Love and Laughter: A Pride and Prejudice Short Stories Anthology

This is a work of fiction based on the works of Jane Austen. All the characters and events portrayed in this novel are products of Jane Austen's original novel or the authors' imaginations.

A GIFT FOR ELIZABETH

Cover Design by Jann Rowland

Published by One Good Sonnet Publishing

ISBN: 9781987929980
ISBN-13: 1987929985

To my family who have, as always, shown
their unconditional love and encouragement.

CHAPTER I

$\mathscr{S}$now was falling. It was not the fine, wind-driven bits of ice which stung the cheeks of those unlucky enough to be walking against the flow of the wind. These flakes were large and fluffy, akin to the down of a goose, lazily floating through the air, alighting on the ground below and instantly rendering it sodden, turning dirt paths into quagmires of mud.

Given the existence of such inclement conditions, one might have suspected those out in it would hurry along, eager to reach home and the warmth promised by a roaring hearth. One would be correct in a general sense. Out on the street beyond the gate, the denizens of the city could be seen hurrying along, the slush of the roads pushed to the sides where their feet fell, leaving footprints which quickly filled again with slurry water and newly fallen snow.

On a bench situated along the path from the massive doors to the gate beyond, sat a young woman. Every so often, the woman would brush at the snow gathering on her lap and shoulders, sending it careening into the air to mingle with the continually falling flakes to join that accumulating on the ground or the bench on which she sat. Perhaps it would be best to go back into the Foundling Hospital, to wait inside, away from the dampening effects of the weather. But the young woman was a hardy soul, one accustomed to walking, often when others might have thought her daft. The wonder of the newly fallen snow and the crispness of the air was not something she would willingly forgo. And it was not as if it was uncomfortably cold either, as the half-melted snow under her feet could attest.

London was not where Miss Elizabeth Bennet had been raised, and while it had been her place of residence for some months now, she still did not consider it her home. Her aunt and uncle, with whom she lived, were everything attentive and kind, and she could never repine their society. But she was, in essence, a country girl, one more suited to walking the paths near her father's estate than the pavement of the large city.

The thought of her erstwhile home brought a lump to Elizabeth's throat and a stinging to her eyes. She was not a woman made for melancholy, however, and she pushed such thoughts from her mind in favor of happier thoughts. She had much of which to be thankful, after all, and the approaching of the Christmas season and the celebration of the Savior's birth was not a time to be unhappy.

So Elizabeth sat and waited, watching the snow fall with a kind of childlike wonder. Snow was a phenomenon to be treasured, to anticipate and enjoy, though she knew her uncle's carriage driver would glance at the sky as he drove, cursing the weather which would make his task more difficult. Elizabeth knew that on the morrow she would almost certainly accompany her little cousins to the park near her uncle's home. Perhaps there might even be enough snow for an impromptu snowball fight to break out. Images from Elizabeth's childhood flashed through her mind, memories of Charlotte Lucas, her friend as a girl, and Charlotte's older brother, Samuel, engaged in pelting each other with the soft balls of snow, as her sisters were usually unwilling to engage in such games.

Elizabeth sighed. It seemed as if thoughts of the past were destined to plague her that evening. Through the haze of the thickly falling ice, Elizabeth wondered what had prevented the carriage from arriving as it had every other day. Her uncle was very good for allowing her this much freedom, making his carriage available to transport her as often as he did. The hospital was a matter of two, perhaps three miles from his house. And while she was happy to hail a hackney instead of burdening her uncle, her funds were limited, and her uncle insisted. But it had never been this late before.

A glance back revealed the solid, imposing form of the Foundling Hospital. Within, Elizabeth knew the children would be partaking of their evening meal, to be sent to their rooms and their beds soon after. In her time working there, she had become quite attached to some of the little girls. Some had even begun to emulate her, their cherub faces shining with pleasure at every little compliment, every kindness she bestowed upon them.

Their situations broke Elizabeth's heart. So many little ones, adrift and alone in the world, never having known the love of a mother, the guidance of a father. Though Elizabeth often felt herself similarly alone, she had been raised in the bosom of a loving family, which, while there were times of trial and vexation, had been the forming of her current character. She could not imagine the pain and suffering of those little ones as they came to the realization that no one in the world loved them as a parent loves a child.

As the night deepened, Elizabeth began to take some thought as to what she might do should the carriage not come, little likely though that seemed. The distance was not one she could not walk—why, she had walked much further in the countryside many times! But London was not Hertfordshire, and there were dangers here which were not present in the country. The city had seemed civilized enough from the window of her uncle's carriage when she had passed through it that morning. But appearances could be deceiving, and a seemingly benevolent face might hide ungentlemanly thoughts and threatening proclivities.

The other option was, of course, to hail a hackney. That course of action was not without its own risks, especially with the night deepening. Elizabeth knew she possessed the means to do so if she chose, but the other occasions in which she had traveled in that manner were undertaken earlier in the day, not in the deepening gloom of night. Who knew what kind of man she might entrust herself to for her transportation?

As the time wore on, Elizabeth knew she must do something, for her aunt and uncle would begin to worry. Perhaps it was best to wait in the hospital? Surely they would become concerned when the carriage did not arrive with her a passenger within. But Elizabeth was not a woman who waited. She was capable and competent, and such a predicament demanded she take charge of her own welfare. And so, with a final look back at the hospital, she determined to rise and be on her way.

The sight of a tall man, imposing against the backdrop of the large building, arrested her motion. He was a tall man, a top hat perched on his head, a wealth of dark curling out from under the brim, framing a stern face in which was set a pair of dark eyes. The man did not look displeased, so much as curious. And in a shock of recognition, Elizabeth realized she had seen him before.

The circumstances which had led to Elizabeth's situation on the bench outside London's Foundling Hospital were not at all unusual. Elizabeth had always been an active sort of person, whether it had been walking, engaging in the society near her home, tending to the tenants of her father's estate, or working with her elder sister on the gardens behind their home or in the small stillroom the estate boasted.

But after several weeks of enforced inactivity at her uncle's house, Elizabeth had been desperate for some occupation to take her mind from her troubles. This restlessness had led to the conversation which had resulted in her taking more of an active role in her own life.

"It is too much!" Elizabeth had exclaimed some weeks before, closing the book which had sat unread in her lap for several fruitless minutes.

"What is, Lizzy?" her aunt had asked. Mrs. Gardiner, by contrast to Elizabeth's restless energy, had continued with her sewing, not even glancing up at Elizabeth's outburst. She had seen Elizabeth's growing discontent, no doubt, for such episodes were becoming more frequent.

"This . . . This sitting in your home, doing nothing as the world passes me by!" Elizabeth pushed her book to the side and stood, pacing the sitting-room with agitated steps. "Surely there must be some occupation, some way in which I may be of some use to *someone*."

At this statement, her aunt did look up with a mixture of fondness and pity. "I would not say you are useless. Your help with the children is a wonderful boon for which I cannot express enough gratitude. And you assist in everything I ask with nary a complaint."

"Who could do anything less?" asked Elizabeth, continuing her pacing. "You are everything that is good, supporting me and allowing me to live in your home. Such repayment is a pitiful gesture, indeed, but it is all I have."

"No repayment is required. You know this."

"I do, Aunt," replied Elizabeth with a sigh. "I love you and Uncle, and I appreciate everything you have done for me." Her nervous energy spent, Elizabeth once again sank down on the sofa. "Do not think I am ungrateful. It is simply . . ."

Elizabeth sighed and turned to look at her aunt, noting her attention was now away from her sewing and fixed on Elizabeth herself. "I feel I have no purpose," said Elizabeth in a soft voice, looking away so she would not choke up at the sight of her aunt's pity. "The gratitude I feel for you and Uncle is profound. But surely there must be more than this.

"My sisters and mother may be content to live in their cottage, mingle with whatever society will have them, and simply allow the years to pass. But I feel I need something more. There *must* be something more to this life."

"Not *all* your sisters live in the cottage."

Once again Elizabeth's throat felt constricted as if choked by a scarf tied too tightly. That subject was even more painful, and Elizabeth shied away from it out of instinct. Unfortunately, what emerged from her mouth was guaranteed to provoke her aunt.

"Perhaps I should go into service."

It was an old argument, even considering the short time in which Elizabeth had resided with the Gardiners. Her aunt was not any more pleased that Elizabeth had brought it up again than she had been any other time the subject had been raised.

"That is not required." There was a firmness in her aunt's tone, one which, had she been a child, would have removed all thoughts of contradiction. "Your uncle and I wish you to stay as long as necessary. And we have many friends—surely your prospects are not so dim as to require your going into service. There must be a man who will value you for what you are, the daughter of a gentleman, even if you do not possess a handsome fortune to tempt him."

Elizabeth loved her aunt's positivity. Unfortunately, she had learned the harsh truth of the world. Perhaps there would be a man to overlook the unfortunate truth of her position, but Elizabeth knew it unlikely she would ever find that man. And that did not even begin to consider her current situation and the situation of her family. Her aunt did not like to hear Elizabeth state as much, but it was nothing less than the truth.

"And what will happen if I do not find a man to marry me?" asked Elizabeth after she had made these points to her aunt. "What shall then become of me? I cannot stay here forever?"

"We would be very happy if you did."

"None of us will live forever, Aunt."

"And if your uncle or I should pass on before you, I am certain our eldest would be happy to keep you, his beloved aunt, under his roof."

Elizabeth shook her head. "Perhaps he might. But I cannot live under such circumstances. You must know this, Aunt. I require something more."

A slow nod was Mrs. Gardiner's response. "There is certainly something to what you say, Lizzy. I cannot fault your desire to make a difference in your life.

"But this talk of going into service is *not* necessary," continued her aunt. Elizabeth frowned, ready to contradict her when Mrs. Gardiner raised her hand for silence. "If you wish to help, I might, perhaps, be in a position to suggest something to give you some occupation. If you are willing."

In spite of herself, Elizabeth's interest was pricked. While she might prefer to embark on providing for herself, she knew her aunt and uncle were adamant that she not do something so demeaning as going into service. In the interest of present harmony, she nodded, indicating that her aunt continue.

"As you are aware, I am engaged in assisting with several charities, some of which I serve as a board member. If you would like, you could provide assistance as a volunteer."

Elizabeth frowned. "Such as the Foundling Hospital?"

"I do not have as much to do with that institution," replied Mrs. Gardiner, "but there are several at which you might assist. None of them would become a source of income for you, of course. But it may assist you in shedding this persistent malaise which seems to have fallen over you."

"I suppose I could make the attempt," said Elizabeth slowly, considering the possibilities.

"You are a good girl, Lizzy," said Mrs. Gardiner, patting her hand, a gesture which bespoke her love and esteem. "Join me when I go to the poorhouse tomorrow. It is a worthy cause and one which will allow you to feel you are useful."

In the end, though Mrs. Gardiner introduced her to several of the charities to which she gifted her time, Elizabeth found herself drawn to the hospital. There was simply something about those little faces that tugged at her heartstrings. In some ways they were much like her cousins, so trusting, so innocent. In other ways, the harshness of the life they had led had aged them before their time, jaded them beyond what young children should be required to endure.

Before long, Elizabeth was spending three days a week assisting at the hospital and would have increased that amount, had her uncle not laughingly protested the continuous use of his carriage. "I am glad you have found some purpose, Lizzy," said her uncle, fixing her with an affectionate smile. "But perhaps a little moderation would be in order, do you not think?"

So Elizabeth acquiesced and limited herself to three days a week. The matter of her suggestion of going into service was pushed to the side for the present. Elizabeth did not forget it, nor did she lose the conviction it would be her ultimate path in life. The Gardiners, for their parts, seemed happy she had relinquished such thoughts. Thus everyone was happy such matters had been pushed to the side.

The night in question was unusual, indeed. Her uncle's carriage had always arrived to retrieve her before the time of her departure and was obliged to wait for her to emerge. Her uncle preferred it this way, for as he had said to her more than once, "It is better for the carriage to arrive early than to keep you waiting in the cold."

But here she was, waiting for a means of conveying her home, which was by now more than thirty minutes late. When the man appeared into her sight, Elizabeth was startled for a moment, but not afraid. She had seen him once or twice about the hospital, and as she possessed a good memory for faces, she recognized him at once. He was not the kind of man who was forgettable, for he stood tall and forbidding, his air and manner stern, his countenance striking, as handsome a man as she had ever seen. And he stood in the courtyard of the hospital, gazing at her with a slight frown. Elizabeth wondered if he thought her to be a loiterer.

Miss Elizabeth Bennet had seen the gentleman in the hospital a time or two, but he had been there many more times when she had *not* seen him. She would have been surprised how much he had observed her since she began working there and even more had she known exactly who he was and what position in society he possessed. In her current circumstances, she might have felt some measure of intimidation at being the focus of the man's scrutiny.

The position he held was an old one. The Foundling Hospital had been established in 1739, and at its inception, his grandfather had been among the board of governors. From that time, the governorship held by his family had been passed to his son, and now to his grandson. Even as a young man and new master of his estate, he had held the position, striving to do the best he could to fulfill his obligations to the best of his abilities.

There had been times, however, when he had felt burdened by the responsibility, just as he was by the other cares which weighed down on him. Surely to care for his estates, donate of his wealth to the poor and needy, to guide his sister in society, and uphold his family name was all that could be expected from one man. At times, he had thought to allow the position to go to another, to refocus his thoughts on other matters which required his attention, his family's history with the place notwithstanding. But something had always held him back, whether it was duty, honor, or simply a nudge from something beyond his understanding, informing him he would one day be glad he had kept the association.

Now, he thought he knew why he had been kept here. The first glimpse he had caught of the young woman had been something akin to a rush of pure fire through his veins. He was not a man to allow himself flights of fancy. He was a man of the world, one who had lived in the midst of society all his life, who had become jaded by the overt greed and grasping nature of his fellow man, particularly those of higher society. How could a man such as he believe in such poetic nonsense of instant love?

Even now he could not state that it *was* love. How could he know? He had not exchanged two words with the young lady. But as he watched her, as he noted her diligence in performing the tasks to which she was set when she gave of her time and energy, he was struck by how pure she seemed, how open and honest she was when connecting to these young unfortunates. By now, he knew, she was adored by the girls she assisted, and more than one of the young boys had been heard to state how they would marry her when they came of age. And he well understood their interest, for she was exquisite, not only in her character but in the beauty of her countenance and in the light of her dark eyes. He had rarely seen a jewel of such worth as she.

It would not do for a man of his standing to be drawn in by a young girl of whom he knew nothing. His was an old family, one connected to several families of the nobility and many more of wealth and position. It would be a scandal of the worst sort should he be captured by a woman who was not, at the very least, of the gentry herself. He knew he could aspire to wed the daughter of an earl, should he choose, little though such a society wife interested him.

Those fears were put to rest by what he had heard when inquiring concerning her. Oh, he was never overt, never direct in his inquiries. He would ask a general question about the volunteers, of whom there were not a few, turning it with subtle questions and general interest to the girl who interested him.

"A good girl, that one," the matron told him not two days before he came across her outside on that dark and snowy night.

"She is new here, is she not?" he had asked, doing his best to appear casual.

"She is," replied the matron. "Mrs. Gardiner, one of the ladies who donates her assistance from time to time, brought her around three weeks ago. She has been a regular ever since. A niece, I believe."

Filing the name Gardiner away for future reference, he replied: "She is from home, then."

"I can't rightly say. Oh, she is not living with her parents at present—that is certain enough. I understand she hails from Hertfordshire, from an estate some distance from the northern edge of town. But I know not much more of her, for she does not speak of herself."

Eager to avoid an unseemly degree of interest, he had allowed the subject to rest. It was nothing less than a fact that he had spent much more time at the hospital since first catching sight of her, especially when he learned the days she preferred to work there. It would not do for whispers to begin among the staff.

So he watched her whenever he had the chance, noting her ease with the children, the way she would engage herself in their games, delighting her charges with her enthusiasm and interest. More than once he had caught himself staring at her when she was engaged in some task, and he thought she had discovered his interest more than once. But if she did, she either did not know who he was, or she was of such a character that she did not try to take advantage of his interest. Either way, his interest in her was further raised.

It was nothing less than the truth that his thoughts were fixed on her that evening as he walked out of the building to meet his sister. But then again, his thoughts were almost always on her of late. Seeing her in the darkening night, watching her look about as if she had never before seen snow, he was charmed all over again. And taking it as providence, he determined to approach her and damn the consequences.

As she turned, her eyes alighting on him with curiosity, but no fear, Fitzwilliam Darcy stepped forward and addressed her.

"Good evening, Miss. Is there something I can do to assist?"

CHAPTER II

A s the sound of his soft baritone reached her ears, Elizabeth found it difficult to believe he had actually spoken to her. What man of his obvious standing would speak to a woman who may be naught but a servant, for all he knew? But lest he think her a simpleton, Elizabeth knew she must respond, though she knew it could be considered improper.

"I thank you, sir. But I am completely well."

He paused for a moment as if considering walking away and leaving her behind. But then his voice reached her ears again, and she was surprised all over again.

"Well you may be, but it appears you are stranded. Why else would you be sitting on a cold bench with snow falling all about?"

Elizabeth could not help but laugh at his words, and before she could still her tongue, an arch reply escaped her lips: "Perhaps I am simply fond of snow."

A smile lit up his countenance, rendering his uncommonly handsome face all the more appealing because of it. "Even those who enjoy the snow usually do not sit while it accumulates around them. If you stay here much longer, one might mistake you for a snowman."

"I doubt that very much, sir. Even now as the snow falls, it melts quickly. It is not nearly cold enough for it to remain with us, even though I might wish it was so."

"Ah, you have caught my exaggeration," was his expansive reply. Then he became serious again. "I hope you do not think I am prying, but it seems to me there is something amiss. Are you waiting for conveyance to your home?"

"Yes," replied Elizabeth. "My uncle sends a carriage to collect me, but tonight it is unusually late. I cannot account for it."

"Then perhaps I might be of assistance," replied the man. "If you are willing, my sister awaits me in my carriage beyond the gate. It would be no trouble to convey you to your uncle's home. The last thing I would wish is to hear you caught a cold because you sat in the cold and damp waiting for a carriage which has been delayed. You do not know how long it will be."

Charmed though she was by this man's offer and his earnestness, Elizabeth could not allow another to put themselves out for her. "I shall be well, I am certain, sir. It is likely as you say — the carriage will be along as soon as the delay has been resolved."

"I beg your pardon, Miss," replied the man, his tone firmer than before, "but I do not believe it is safe for a young woman to remain alone, even within this courtyard. Shall I summon my sister to reassure you I mean no harm?"

"I never suspected you of ulterior motives," replied Elizabeth, feeling the heat rise in her cheeks. "I merely do not wish to be a burden."

"It seems impossible you could ever be a burden, Miss . . ."

It was an invitation to introduce herself. Elizabeth was well enough acquainted with society in general, and with higher society, of which she thought this man to be a member, to know that introducing oneself to another without the benefit of a mutual acquaintance would be frowned upon. Yet, she could do nothing but respond.

"Elizabeth Bennet, sir. I am originally of Hertfordshire, though I have been living with my aunt and uncle these past months."

Something crossed the man's countenance, something Elizabeth could not quite name. It seemed similar to a scent which tickled the nose, but one which he could not quite place, or the face of a person one has seen before, but cannot quite remember where. It seemed her name was not unknown to him, though his eyes did not light up with immediate recognition.

But he did not hesitate to reciprocate in introducing himself to her acquaintance: "Fitzwilliam Darcy, of Pemberley in Derbyshire, at your service."

If her name had been known to him, his was doubly so to her. The recognition must have been evident on her countenance, for he nodded and spoke yet again.

"It seems we possess a common connection, Miss Bennet," said he. Then his countenance darkened, and he continued: "Or, at least a *former* connection. But I do not believe the teeth of inclement weather is the place to have such a conversation. Shall we not proceed? I shall ask those at the hospital to inform your driver that you have proceeded to your uncle's house, should he arrive."

Though very aware it would probably be best if she demurred, Elizabeth found she could not refuse this man's kind offer. She gave him her consent, after which Mr. Darcy stepped back into the building to leave his instructions. Then he returned to escort her toward his carriage.

His conveyance was located around the corner of the entrance wall, out of sight from her previous position on the bench. Elizabeth was so surprised by what she saw that she almost stopped walking in her shock. The carriage was enormous, its costly nature evident in the fineness of the craftsmanship, the large springs which promised a far smoother ride than any she had ever experienced, the black lacquered exterior, and the crest painted on the back. It was pulled by four carriage horses, beasts which had been chosen due to their sleek, powerful frames built for endurance and, presumably, for their matching appearance and abilities. As they approached, one of the lead horses snorted and stamped its greeting.

"Please excuse me for a moment, Miss Bennet," said Mr. Darcy, disengaging his arm from hers as he moved toward the door of the coach. "I shall inform my sister of the increase of our party."

He stepped forward and, opening the door, stuck his head inside, speaking quietly for a few moments. Then a young lady stepped down from the coach and approached her, eyes curiously lowered. Miss Darcy was a tall young lady, her blonde hair gathered around the edges of her bonnet, her eyes indistinct due to the fact that she did not look up. Elizabeth judged her age as younger than twenty, based on what she could see. Given what she had heard of this young lady, she knew Miss Darcy was closer to seventeen or eighteen years of age.

"Miss Bennet," said Mr. Darcy, leading his sister toward her, "please allow me to introduce you to my sister. Georgiana, this is Miss Elizabeth Bennet of Hertfordshire, though she has been recently staying in London with her aunt and uncle. Miss Bennet, my sister,

Georgiana Darcy."

The ladies curtseyed to each other, yet Miss Darcy did not look up. Though she would not have expected it, Elizabeth found herself suddenly certain that Miss Darcy was exceedingly shy. Thus, it fell to her to attempt to induce the other girl to comfort.

"Good evening, Miss Darcy. Please allow me to thank you for sharing your coach with me this evening. My uncle's carriage must have been delayed, for it has usually arrived by this time."

"It is no trouble, Miss Bennet," came the girl's quiet reply. Then she seemed to gather her courage, for she hazarded a look up and said: "Does your uncle live far from here?"

"About two or three miles," was Elizabeth's reply. "I have walked that distance when I lived at my childhood home, but in London, it seems ill-advised at best. My uncle would not forgive me should I enter his house having walked through the city."

"Your uncle is a wise man," said Mr. Darcy. "But I think we should depart and attend to our discussion in the carriage. Might I inquire as to your uncle's address, Miss Bennet?"

Elizabeth told him and waited as he gave the instructions to his driver. Then Mr. Darcy helped first his sister, then Elizabeth into the waiting carriage. She took her seat next to Miss Darcy, as was proper, and when Mr. Darcy entered, the conveyance lurched into motion.

"Now that we are on our way," said Mr. Darcy, not wasting any time, "perhaps we should satisfy each other's curiosity concerning our shared connection."

It seemed Miss Darcy forgot her reticence, for she blurted: "Connection?" The manner in which she glanced at Elizabeth out of the corner of her eyes suggested she suspected her of some nefarious plan of entrapping her brother. And so she should, thought Elizabeth; she might feel the same, were she in the girl's shoes.

"And yet you termed it a *former connection*," rejoined Elizabeth. "I find that I am rather curious."

"Former in the sense that I have not seen or spoken with Bingley for some time," replied Mr. Darcy. "Am I correct in assuming you are sister to the Miss Bennet who married my friend Bingley last year?"

"I am," replied Elizabeth. There were other matters concerning that connection of which she should probably inform him, but the task seemed daunting at present.

Mr. Darcy nodded. "I had thought as much. Though if pressed I would still call Bingley a friend, our friendship was strained by . . . an event which occurred more than a year ago. I have not seen Bingley since that time, and as he has never been a good correspondent, we have not kept in contact.

"I have, however, heard rumors of his marriage, enough to have heard the name of his new wife. Those mutual friends who have made her acquaintance have been universal in their approbation."

"If there is anyone in the world who could disapprove of my sister," said Elizabeth quietly, "I have yet to meet them. There is no sweeter or more angelic woman in the world than my sister."

"Very beautiful too, if what I have heard is correct."

"The very best of us all," replied Elizabeth. "If you consider your friendship with Mr. Bingley intact, I dare say he shares your sentiment tenfold."

The siblings shared a low chuckle, one which Elizabeth understood. Mr. Bingley was about as inoffensive a person as she had ever met, his affectionate nature not allowing him to disapprove of anyone. If only . . .

"That does not surprise me, Miss Bennet," said Mr. Darcy. "Bingley has ever been a good friend, and while we disagreed, I do not hold it against him or accuse him of anything improper. It has been my wish that the gulf between us be repaired."

"Then should you approach him, you would not find him disinclined to hear you." Elizabeth paused and laughed. "When he came to Hertfordshire last year, he was eager to inform everyone of his very good friend. I dare say you are the best and most knowledgeable master of your estate, the truest and staunchest friend, and the most upright man in all of England."

"Bingley does, of course, exaggerate."

"Even if he does," replied Elizabeth, "if half of what he says is true, you are a true paragon of virtue, sir." Then Elizabeth turned to Miss Darcy. "And your name is not unknown to me either, Miss Darcy. Mr. Bingley's sister was eager to praise you as her bosom friend, a most poised, elegant, and accomplished young woman."

A shadow passed over the faces of both Darcys, telling Elizabeth that Miss Bingley had likely had some influence on the disagreement between the two men. Elizabeth had known Miss Bingley was social climber the moment they had been introduced—she never would have given up the friendship of such people if given a choice. Her continual praise of the Darcys suggested she was eager to restore it, should the opportunity ever present itself.

"You must not give credence to everything Miss Bingley says," said Miss Darcy. "In actuality, I do not know her well. She is the sister of my brother's friend and has always been eager to praise me, whether praise was warranted or no."

"Believe me, Miss Darcy," said Elizabeth, "I was certain I took Miss Bingley's measure very quickly in our acquaintance. I am certain you are no less estimable regardless."

The hesitant smile with which Miss Darcy regarded her suggested a lessening of the girl's reticence. For his part, Mr. Darcy did not seem to be angered by her less than reverent words concerning his friend's sister. Elizabeth was more certain than ever that Miss Bingley had done something to earn Mr. Darcy's ire.

"Do you plan to be in London during the Christmas season, Miss Bennet?" asked Miss Darcy, apparently uncomfortable with the previous topic of conversation.

For her part, Elizabeth felt the new subject was as awkward as the first, but she essayed to respond nonetheless. "I believe my residence in London is to be of some duration, though I suspect some change in the New Year."

"We are to be here as well," said Mr. Darcy, apparently sensing Elizabeth's discomfort. "We will often spend it at our home in the north. But this year I have certain business concerns which require me to be in town. My presence at the Foundling Hospital today was in part to escape from those concerns."

"Is there anything amiss, Mr. Darcy?" asked Elizabeth, sensing something in his manner which suggested concern.

"Nothing of import," replied he, perhaps a little too glibly. "They are more time-consuming matters, which I would prefer to dispense with. But I must look after them, for they are healthy concerns."

Elizabeth nodded slowly. "My uncle is quite knowledgeable about such things. If you wish, I can introduce you to him. I am certain he would be happy to assist with whatever knowledge he possesses."

"Thank you, Miss Bennet," said Mr. Darcy. "I would like that."

It took a moment for Elizabeth to realize what she had done. Many would consider it an impertinence to offer to introduce a man of business to a man who was as prominent in society as she suspected Mr. Darcy was. But the man gave no impression of offense. And Elizabeth realized that if he claimed as a friend Mr. Bingley—who was by his own confession the son of a tradesman—he must have no particular distaste for men who earn their bread by means of trade.

Before Elizabeth could respond, there arose a commotion outside the carriage, and their motion slowed and soon stopped. His attention caught, Mr. Darcy leaned his head out the window and spoke to the driver, the man's words muffled. When he re-entered the carriage, Mr. Darcy smiled at Elizabeth and said:

"It seems the mystery of your uncle's missing carriage has been solved, Miss Bennet."

Curious as to his meaning, Elizabeth followed him as he stepped out the door, and when she alighted on the street beside him with his assistance, his meaning became clear. On the other side of the street, a disturbance had halted traffic, with several carriages lined up behind one which sat at a precarious angle, a rear wheel broken into splinters. There, beside the conveyance, looking stressed, stood Jacobs, her uncle's driver. When he noticed her presence, he appeared to deflate with relief. He approached and addressed her.

"I am sorry, Miss Bennet, but as you can see, we have had a spot of trouble."

"I can see that, Jacobs," replied Elizabeth. "No one was hurt?"

"No, Miss. I sent George ahead to the hospital to inform you of the situation and convey you to the master's house."

"As you can see, Mr. Darcy has kindly offered to convey me home."

The driver turned his eyes on Mr. Darcy, his eyes assessing, as if wondering if it was advisable to entrust his master's beloved niece with a stranger. The bearing and obvious standing of the man before him brought him quickly to the correct answer, for he pressed his knuckles to his forehead.

"I thank you, sir. I was worried for the miss's safety."

"She is entirely safe with me," Mr. Darcy. "My sister also accompanies us in my carriage."

Jacobs nodded and said: "Then I will not worry about her. I hope George returns soon, for something must be done about Mr. Gardiner's carriage."

"We left word at the hospital," said Elizabeth.

"Then I will leave you in the gentleman's capable hands."

Then Jacobs bowed and returned to the carriage, while Elizabeth was escorted back to Mr. Darcy's carriage. He assisted her in, then had a word with his driver, before embarking, and they were off once again. When they were underway, he turned to Elizabeth.

"As I recall, there is a carriage maker in this part of town. One of my footmen will stay with your driver and assist him in having it repaired."

"Thank you, sir," said Elizabeth, wondering at this man's generosity.

Seeing her look, Mr. Darcy misinterpreted it, he said: "There is nothing with which to concern yourself, Miss Bennet. I am certain Mr. Gardiner's carriage will be repaired quickly."

"I hope so, sir. It will be difficult to make my way to the hospital without it."

"How often do you go?" asked Miss Darcy.

"Three times every week at present," replied Elizabeth. She paused and smiled at Miss Darcy. "If I could persuade my uncle, I would go more often. But he is adamant that three times a week is enough."

"Does he not require the use of his own carriage?" asked Mr. Darcy.

"At times," replied Elizabeth, "when he has meetings in another part of town or when my aunt and uncle participate in society. But uncle lives close enough to his offices that he can walk. That is why he lives in the part of town he does, as he finds it quite convenient."

The information seemed to impress Mr. Darcy, as he smiled and nodded. They passed the rest of the journey in pleasant, though banal, conversation, carried primarily by Elizabeth and Mr. Darcy. Miss Darcy, Elizabeth could see, made an effort to participate. But it was equally evident that she was quite painfully shy, and often, though she appeared like she wished to say something, she found herself unequal to the task. Elizabeth attempted to include her as much as she could, an effort both Darcys seemed to appreciate, though she was not certain as to the level of her success.

At length, the house on Gracechurch Street wove into view, and the coach pulled to a stop. With a few words for his sister to await him in the carriage—which Elizabeth thought was for the best, given her shyness—Mr. Darcy helped Elizabeth from the coach and, offering his arm to her, escorted her up the stairs to her uncle's door. Before they had crossed the distance, the door flew open, and Mrs. Gardiner appeared, her countenance etched with worry.

"Lizzy!" exclaimed she. "I was worried when you did not appear at your usual time!"

"Uncle's carriage suffered a broken wheel," said Elizabeth by way of explanation, accepting her aunt's worried embrace. "Mr. Darcy was kind enough to offer me transportation."

"My sister is in the carriage as well," said Mr. Darcy quickly, eager to reassure Mrs. Gardiner that the proprieties had been observed.

Mrs. Gardiner, for her part, seemed more than a little surprised at the mention of the gentleman's name. She regarded him for a moment, clearly choosing her words carefully, before addressing him.

"I beg your pardon, sir, but are you perhaps related to the Darcys of Pemberley?"

It was as if a shutter was pulled over a window, as Mr. Darcy's look became closed. He did not deny it, but his answer was soft and wary.

"Your estate is very beautiful, sir," said Mrs. Gardiner. "When I was a girl, my father was the rector at Lambton, with which I am sure you must be familiar."

"I am!" exclaimed Mr. Darcy. "Why, Lambton is not five minutes from Pemberley."

"A fact of which I am well aware, sir."

"Then you must be the daughter of Mr. Plumber," said Mr. Darcy slowly, his face lined with thought.

"Yes," said Mrs. Gardiner. "Furthermore, my grandfather was the master of Ash Park, the estate now held by his son, who is my mother's brother."

"That is a curious connection, indeed," said Mr. Darcy. "I never would have thought I would meet someone so well acquainted with my neighborhood here in London. I do not know the Stewart family well, as their estate is a little further to the east. But they have a good reputation in the area."

What might have been an awkward meeting was thus transformed, as Mr. Darcy and Mrs. Gardiner exchanged some few words, comparing their news of the neighborhood as well as some common acquaintances and knowledge of places. The sudden reticence in Mr. Darcy's manner when Elizabeth's aunt had first questioned him was gone, and he seemed easy in her company. Elizabeth watched with astonishment, saying very little, allowing the others to carry the conversation.

"I apologize, Mrs. Gardiner," said Mr. Darcy at length, "but my sister awaits me in the carriage. I have enjoyed our conversation."

"No more than I, Mr. Darcy. It is not often I have such timely news of the neighborhood."

Mrs. Gardiner paused, her eyes darting between Elizabeth and Mr. Darcy, and had it been Elizabeth's mother, she would have been concerned that something improper was about to issue forth from her mouth. There was no such need to worry with her aunt, though Elizabeth wondered if she was not seeing more into the situation than was warranted.

In the end, it was Mr. Darcy who spoke first. "Pardon me, Mrs. Gardiner, but Miss Bennet mentioned that your husband is knowledgeable about certain subjects of which I find myself in need of expertise. Would it be possible to beg a little of Mr. Gardiner's time?"

Again it seemed Mrs. Gardiner was caught by surprise, but she recovered quickly. "At present, I do not know my husband's schedule, but if you send a note, I will ensure he receives it."

"Thank you, Mrs. Gardiner." Then Mr. Darcy turned to Elizabeth and favored her with a smile which almost stopped her heart. Then he bowed over her hand. "Until next time, Miss Bennet."

Then Mr. Darcy excused himself, leaving the two women watching as his long stride carried him from the house. Elizabeth could not quite decide what she felt at that moment, though a glance at her companion showed her bemusement. But she knew she could expect to be the recipient of a copious amount of teasing in the near future.

"Well, Lizzy, I must own to a certain amount of surprise." She turned and, winding her arm in Elizabeth's, steered her toward the parlor. "Come. You must tell me about the handsome gentleman who just graced my home. Can I assume I will be invited to the wedding?"

CHAPTER III

*E*mbarrassment was a state with which Elizabeth was intimately familiar in the next few days. Elizabeth had long known she inhabited the position of their favorite niece, and she knew they would never be unkind. But Mrs. Gardiner's statements immediately after Mr. Darcy's departure were pointed, and once her uncle learned of the matter, he joined in the gentle poking at his niece.

"Mr. Darcy, is it?" His smile showed his jovial nature, his love shining through in the amusement of his eyes. "I never would have thought such an illustrious man would cross the threshold of my door. It would be best if you were to find a husband for your protection, Lizzy, but perhaps you might set your sights a little lower than a man of the standing and consequence of Mr. Darcy."

Cheeks flaming, Elizabeth opened her mouth to deflect her uncle's comment, but her aunt spoke before she could. "Nothing but the best for our Lizzy, Edward. I shall expect an invitation for next Christmas, my dear. Though I have seen Pemberley's grounds and a little of the house, to actually stay in such a grand house would be something, indeed!"

"Mr. Darcy merely took pity on me when he saw I was stranded!" squeaked Elizabeth, finally able to speak over her relations' teasing. "I doubt I will see him again."

"Do not forget," said Mrs. Gardiner, "that he intends to call on your uncle."

"My *uncle*," stressed Elizabeth. "That has nothing to do with me."

"A convenient excuse," said Mrs. Gardiner, waving Elizabeth's comments away as if they were of no concern. "Mark my words, Lizzy, he will be only too happy to greet you too. There was something in his eyes when he looked at you. I have seen it before, not only in Jane's excellent Mr. Bingley, but also in the eyes of my own dear husband when he looks at me. Mr. Darcy saw you more than as an unfortunate to whom he might extend his charity. I believe his interest is much deeper."

"While I have every confidence in our Lizzy's ability to attract a man's interest," observed Mr. Gardiner, "to do so as quickly as you suggest would be a feat, indeed."

"Certainly not," grumbled Elizabeth, by now becoming cross with their unrelenting words. "I never met him before tonight, and I will not expect anything from him on so short an acquaintance."

"I can see you have tired of our jesting, Lizzy," said Mrs. Gardiner, patting Elizabeth's cheek in a sign of affection. "I shall not sport with you any longer. But I will say that I *did* detect interest in his manner. Whether anything will come of it, I cannot say." Then she leaned in and in a voice soft, yet audible to her more distance husband, she said: "He is frightfully handsome, is he not?"

Had Elizabeth managed to refrain from blushing, she might have avoided the laughter of her aunt and uncle. The heat in her cheeks testified to her failure in that regard, and their mirth flowed freely. Elizabeth was grateful they refrained thereafter, and the evening was spent happily in company with those she loved most.

Having had no time to consider the matter in advance, Darcy was not certain what he might have expected from the home of a tradesman. The evening he had delivered Miss Bennet to the house, he had possessed little opportunity to take his impression of the place. The façade was pleasant and clean, the entrance neat, if not large. The woman who had met them at the door had been genteel, no doubt due to her upbringing as the daughter of a parson, the granddaughter of a gentleman.

Of the master of the house, Darcy had few expectations. Darcy had enough experience with men of Mr. Gardiner's station to know that most were good men, some possessing the manners necessary to pass themselves off as gentry, while there were a few, inevitably, who were rough and coarse. The man's wife suggested Mr. Gardiner was not one of the latter, but Darcy decided he would reserve judgment.

Darcy's note was dispatched the following morning, a reply received that afternoon, and a time for Darcy's visit agreed upon for two hours after noon the following day. When Darcy arrived at the house, he was immediately shown into the master's study, and while he might have wished to catch a glimpse of Miss Bennet, she was nowhere in evidence.

The man of the house was of average height, perhaps ten years Darcy's senior, with an open, jovial countenance, and a hearty welcome. He was, perhaps, a little portly, though it was also obvious he was an active man, and his hair was full upon his head, only greying a little at the temples. His greeting was almost as welcoming as Bingley's might have been in a similar situation.

"Mr. Darcy, I presume," said Mr. Gardiner, extending his hand for Darcy to shake. "Welcome, sir. Given all my wife has said of her recollection of your estate and the neighborhood in which you live, I never thought I would actually make your acquaintance. I am happy for it, regardless."

"Thank you, sir," replied Darcy, accepting his hand, impressed with the firmness of Mr. Gardiner's handshake. "I am quite happy to make your acquaintance as well. In fact, I am hoping I will derive immediate benefit from your expertise, for your niece informed me of your knowledge of matters of business."

"I will assist as much as I am able, of course," replied Mr. Gardiner. "What seems to be the trouble?"

Mr. Gardiner was more than Darcy had ever hoped. When Darcy explained his concerns with a number of his investments, referring to a pair of portfolios he had brought for the purpose, Mr. Gardiner showed his acumen by not only being familiar with them but explaining in greater detail the finer points, and even recommending he divest himself of one of the interests which had most concerned Darcy. Mr. Gardiner was also good enough to suggest another of which he was aware that Darcy could use to take its place. Within a half hour of his coming, Darcy felt much more comfortable with his investments and with the ultimate success of his endeavors.

"I must own that I had not, even given your niece's praise, expected to find such understanding as you have shown, sir," said Darcy, sitting back in his chair.

"One cannot spend more than a decade in business and not learn from experience," replied Mr. Gardiner. Then he laughed. "Or perhaps it is more correct to state that any man of business who does *not* learn such things will soon find himself bankrupt."

"I have no doubt of it," replied Darcy, feeling at ease with this man. Developing a rapport so quickly with anyone of such a brief acquaintance was unusual for Darcy, though he did not question his good fortune. "Nonetheless, I thank you for listening to me, a stranger, and assisting me to the extent you have."

"It is nothing. I am more than happy to impart of what I know when the opportunity presents itself." Mr. Gardiner paused, his gaze fixed on Darcy, his manner thoughtful. "In fact, you might consider it repayment for your kindness to my niece. Lizzy is a sensible girl and would undoubtedly have managed without your assistance. But a young woman alone in the city is a target for those unsavory elements, and your actions relieved me from the need to discover the extent of her resiliency."

"Who would have done less? I was happy to help. In the process, I learned we share a curious connection, and one which I never would have expected to realize."

"Yes, your friend's marriage to my niece. Lizzy informed me of the connection. I understand, however, that your friendship has lapsed?"

There was a probing quality in Mr. Gardiner's voice which Darcy instantly understood, and would have expected, had he thought of the matter in any great detail. He was reluctant to speak of his private affairs in detail, but he knew the man deserved to understand the basics of the matter. He *was* responsible for his niece, after all.

"It is true I have not spoken to Bingley in some time," said Darcy. "For my part, however, I still consider him a friend, regardless of our disagreement, and I expect he is of a similar mind. It is only that Bingley is not an easy man with whom to share a correspondence. Deciphering his letters should be a course taught at university for those who would hazard a friendship with him."

Mr. Gardiner broke out in laughter. "I shall take your word for it, sir, as I have never received a letter from him."

His mirth subsided, and Mr. Gardiner once again descended to seriousness. "Let me be frank with you, Mr. Darcy. That it is too early for me to play the stern guardian to a young woman I well understand. You have made no overtures, and I am not in a position to demand anything of you regardless.

"Let me simply state that my niece has suffered these past months and has only just begun to recover her spirits. I would never presume to accuse you of improper intentions. But I would request that you take care in your dealings with her. She gives the appearance of strength, but I suspect she is far more fragile at present than you suspect."

It *was* early to be having such a conversation, but given what he was being told, Darcy was not surprised the man had raised the subject. While he had always considered himself a careful, rational man, Darcy felt all rationality leave him when faced with the prospect of the allure of a woman in whose company he had spent all of an hour. Thus, he hastened to reassure Mr. Gardiner.

"You need have no concern that I will impinge upon your niece's peace of mind, Mr. Darcy. In fact, if I raise any expectations, they will not be ones I am reluctant to fulfill."

Mr. Gardiner's eyebrows disappeared into his hair. "But you have only just made her acquaintance."

"I promise nothing at this time, Mr. Gardiner. But even sixty minutes in Miss Bennet's company has taught me that she is a rare gem. Any man would be fortunate to gain her affections."

"Then perhaps you would like to greet her before you depart?"

The sly question prompted Darcy's laughter. "Indeed, I would!"

Miss Bennet was as bright and alluring as Darcy had remembered from two days before. She was sitting with her aunt in the Gardiners' parlor, embroidering while her aunt was sewing. Both ladies looked up when they entered, Miss Bennet with surprise, while Mrs. Gardiner possessed an air of smugness about her that Darcy could not quite understand. Then Miss Bennet rose, prompting Darcy's approach, and all such thoughts fled.

"Miss Bennet," said Darcy, bowing over her hand. "Mrs. Gardiner," he intoned, greeting the lady of the house. "I trust you are both well?"

"Very well, Mr. Darcy," said Mrs. Gardiner. "Was your business completed to your satisfaction?"

"It was. Your husband is a treasure, Mrs. Gardiner. He possessed exactly the knowledge of which I had need. I am fortunate to have made your acquaintance."

"No more fortunate than we," said she. "Will you not stay for tea?"

Darcy agreed and sat near to Miss Bennet. It seemed for a moment that the bright, openness of Miss Bennet's behavior had closed, like a tulip closing at the onset of night. She seemed almost embarrassed to see him, though Darcy had rather thought her as prepossessed a lady as he had ever met. The conversation was carried in a desultory fashion for some minutes until Darcy found a subject which elicited a response.

"Do you go to the hospital again soon, Miss Bennet? As I have been there several times myself in recent weeks, I thought I had seen you there several times."

Miss Bennet hazarded a glance at her uncle, one filled with meaning, and then turned back to him, her hesitation forgotten for the moment. "These past three weeks it has been my practice to go every Monday, Wednesday, and Saturday. But I cannot go tomorrow, as my uncle's carriage has not yet been repaired."

"You may cease to upbraid me with your eyes, Lizzy," said Mr. Gardiner. "The carriage will not be ready until Tuesday, so there is nothing to be done. Fortunately, I have only one appointment in another part of town before that date, and may hire a hackney myself to go to it."

"I could hire a hackney for myself," rejoined Elizabeth.

"That is true, but I prefer to avoid it whenever possible. In my own carriage, I can ensure your safety. A hackney is a riskier prospect."

Though it was clear Miss Bennet understood Mr. Gardiner's reluctance, it was also evident she was not happy to be thus denied. Seeing an opportunity to ensure he continued to be in her company, Darcy spoke up.

"If it is agreeable, I would be happy to convey Miss Bennet to the hospital tomorrow in my coach. My sister and I had planned to go regardless, and to stop here on the way to the hospital would not be any trouble."

Once again Mr. Gardiner's considering eyes found Darcy, but this time his wife was a match for her husband's scrutiny. Miss Bennet, to whom the invitation had been tendered, looked on him with surprise and no little measure of hope. Darcy could not help but wonder at it—why was her time at the hospital so important as this?

"We would not wish to inconvenience you, sir," said Mr. Gardiner.

"It is no inconvenience at all," replied Darcy. "My usual path to the hospital from my home is not far from this street. It would be the work of a moment to stop here to retrieve Miss Bennet. We would, of course, return her here at the end of the day."

Mr. Gardiner's eyes found Miss Bennet. He could see her eagerness as clearly as Darcy could, himself. After a few moments, he assented, thanking Darcy. They arranged a time when Darcy would arrive, and soon it was settled.

The tea arrived soon after, and after Mrs. Gardiner served the company, the Gardiners withdrew to themselves, leaving Darcy with Miss Elizabeth. He spent the rest of the time in their parlor in her excellent company, speaking of a variety of topics. So engrossed was Darcy in their conversation that it was another hour before he departed. He had not realized the passage of time. When in Miss Bennet's presence, something so inconsequential as time could do nothing to intrude upon his senses.

"I seem to remember hearing of your proficiency, Miss Darcy. But I must own that even the excessive praise I heard attributed to you has fallen short of the reality."

By this time, Elizabeth was certain Miss Darcy would catch the tone of her jest. And so it was, for the girl laughed, colored a little, but then rolled her eyes wryly, as Elizabeth had intended.

"Miss Bingley has much to say, I have little doubt. But she has heard me play but once, met me only a handful of times, and yet the way she has always spoken in town according to reports made to my brother, she speaks to anyone who will listen of her friendship with me."

"You have painted her portrait with exactness," replied Elizabeth. "I would have expected nothing less."

Smiling, Miss Darcy turned away to pick up a doll, one which had been overlooked when they had cleaned the room. Seeing the reception the younger girl had received by the children of the hospital, Elizabeth had been heartened to learn she was not unknown to them. Whether brother and sister had actually meant to come to the hospital that day, at least she had come for the first time because her brother had insisted. Elizabeth had feared that it had been nothing more than a convenient excuse to once again be in her company, though the thought *was* flattering.

"They are dear children, are they not?" asked Miss Darcy as she assisted Elizabeth in tidying the playroom in which they had entertained the children that afternoon.

"Indeed," was Elizabeth's soft reply. "I have become attached to them in the short time I have known them." Then she smiled at Miss Darcy and indicated the small pianoforte in the corner of the room. "Teaching them to play simple songs appears to have been a success. No doubt they will request more of your time the next time you are here for that purpose."

"And I am happy to do it. Music is one of the things I truly love. I am always happy to practice my pianoforte."

"It shows in your playing," replied Elizabeth. "If I practiced half so diligently as you, I would play much better than I do."

"I suspect you do not play nearly so ill as you suggest. Perhaps we could meet at my brother's house some day and practice together."

It was an overture of friendship, Elizabeth was certain, delivered with all the diffidence of a girl who was shy and afraid of rejection. Elizabeth was charmed, for Miss Darcy was such a pleasant, unassuming young lady. While she knew it might be better to demur, she could not disappoint the girl in such a way. Besides, Elizabeth wanted a friend for herself. Friends had been in short supply of late.

"I would like that, very much, Miss Darcy."

A beaming smile of pure happiness was Miss Darcy's response. They continued to speak in companionable tones as they tidied the room, discussing this day or that, and finally fixing on Thursday the following week. By then her uncle's carriage would be repaired, and she knew he would be eager to see her deepening her friendship with the Darcys.

When their tasks of setting the children's playroom to rights was complete, the two girls left the room, knowing Mr. Darcy would be waiting for their departure soon after. The afternoon had passed quickly, as such times when enjoyment was to be had were wont to do. Elizabeth was grateful Mr. Darcy had made his offer, for she knew she would have brooded at her uncle's home had she been denied. The ability to lose herself in the service of these children was a balm to her sometimes troubled soul. Elizabeth could not be more grateful.

"How long do you mean to be in town, Miss Bennet?"

With one question, Elizabeth's contentment of mind was disturbed, bring memories of the past with it. Miss Darcy seemed to notice nothing, her innocent question meaning nothing more than what she had stated. Though Elizabeth would have wished to avoid the subject altogether, she could do nothing but respond.

"I shall be here for some time yet, Miss Darcy. I live at my uncle's house at present."

"I am happy to hear it," said Miss Darcy, her naiveté not allowing her to see anything other than the pleasure of continuing to be in Elizabeth's company. "I have not had many friends. I hope you will not consider me impertinent for considering *you* as a friend."

"Of course not!" said Elizabeth. "It is nothing less than I feel for you."

Miss Darcy beamed. "Then I hope you will do the honor of referring to me by my given name."

"The honor is all mine," replied Elizabeth. "When addressing me, you may wish to use the diminutive 'Lizzy.' It has been my name for as long as I can remember."

The pleasure with which the other girl regarded her could not be feigned. She chattered on for some minutes, her pleasure at the solemnizing of their friendship far from being exhausted in her words. Elizabeth listened, her own amusement and pleasure growing. She had not thought to pierce this girl's reserve so quickly.

"Then I shall do so," said Georgiana happily. "I never would have thought to gain a friend with such haste, especially since my ability to gain friends in the past has been particularly inept."

"Ah, but you have enjoyed the friendship of the estimable Miss Caroline Bingley, have you not?"

Georgiana's nose wrinkled as if some unpleasant smell had reached it, and then she laughed delightedly. "That is what I have learned to appreciate about you, Lizzy. You always have some quip to share which will not fail to make me laugh." Georgiana then became pensive. "But surely you have recognized that I am rather reticent. It has always been difficult for me to gain friends, though in school there were a few ladies with whom I was friendly. I have trouble discerning whether they are interested in me, or they merely consider me a path to my brother."

"I can see how that would be confusing," said Elizabeth.

"It is. And my dowry does not help."

A shadow passed over Georgiana's face, and she fell silent. Though Elizabeth could not imagine what might have happened to make this girl so wary of others, she supposed that a handsome dowry must be a powerful inducement for a man to feign feelings he did not possess to gain control of it. It was a small glimpse into another world, one of which Elizabeth had never thought previously. Though much might have been made easier had she and her sisters possessed fortunes of their own, there were even drawbacks to the possession of such worldly security.

"But you concern yourself with none of those things," said Georgiana, recovering from her sudden silence. "I do not see in you the light of avarice which often shines in the eyes of others."

"I should hope not," said Elizabeth. "It is best to look for the content of others' characters, rather than fixing on their worldly goods. We are told not to envy or covet, are we not?"

"Yes," replied Georgiana. She paused and then grinned at Elizabeth, who could see an echo of the Gardiners' teasing in her countenance. Her next words confirmed Elizabeth's suppositions. "It is particularly fortunate, as my brother has often found himself hunted by ladies of society for his position. In you, he need not have such fears."

"No," replied Elizabeth.

"It is ironic," continued Miss Darcy, an entirely feigned blitheness in her manner, "that the one woman who interests him will not accept him because of his position. He has never had to court the favor of young ladies before—they have all been favorably disposed to him when they learned who he was. He will need to work to earn your regard."

Elizabeth stopped walking and faced Georgiana, who had also stopped, looking at her with innocence written on her brow. "I expect no such attention, Georgiana, and I beg you would not tease me. The friendship you and your brother have offered me is enough."

"Which is why I already feel you are such a good friend, Lizzy," replied Georgiana. "But I know my brother. Trust me—he has shown more interest in you in only a few short days than in any other young lady in all his years in society. Had he behaved toward any of *them* as he does to you, they would have ordered their trousseaux. Or do you think Miss Bingley would have remained coy had he shown her even a hint of interest?"

The thought prompted a giggle to escape from Elizabeth's lips. Georgiana just grinned, and Elizabeth scowled in response.

"No doubt she would, Georgiana. But as I said, I am content with your friendship. I have no hope of anything more."

"Georgiana! Miss Bennet!"

The voice of Mr. Darcy startled Elizabeth, and she looked up to see him striding toward them, a grin etched upon his face. It became him very well, Elizabeth decided, for she suspected he was of a serious disposition, which must make every smile he showed all the more precious because of its rarity.

As he approached, Georgiana leaned toward Elizabeth and whispered in her ear: "Perhaps you do not hope for more. But I assure you that I do."

And with these shocking words, she greeted her brother, who asked after their time with the children. Elizabeth, stilled as she was by

Georgiana's words, allowed her friend to make the responses to Mr. Darcy's queries. She watched him as they conversed, wondering at Georgiana's words, trying to see Mr. Darcy's feelings in his actions. Inside, she was as uncomfortable as she had ever been. The thought of his attentions made her feel weak inside. But there were other matters of which he had no knowledge, matters which would make any pursuit of her difficult at best.

Chapter IV

"What say you, Miss Bennet?"

Startled by the sudden question, Elizabeth gaped at Mr. Darcy. The sound of his voice, so melodic and deep, coupled with the sheer presence of his person, had lulled her to complacency, and even as she walked beside him in the park near the Gardiners' home, she felt herself floating with contentment.

"I apologize, Mr. Darcy," managed Elizabeth after a few expectant moments, "but I seem to have been woolgathering. Can I trouble you to repeat your question?"

With a smile, Mr. Darcy patted her hand on his arm, sending frissons of pleasure up her arm, and did just that. Soon they were discussing one of his favorite literary works, which he had recently had occasion to re-read upon learning it was also a favorite of *hers*. Elizabeth, though she attempted to pay more attention to what he was saying, still found herself drifting along the warm currents of his voice. For a girl who had always considered herself so level-headed, she almost felt like Lydia in the company of the officers of the regiment!

More than once, Georgiana had commented on how reticent he was, how he had difficulty speaking with those with whom he was not acquainted, how he at times found himself giving offense where none was intended. But Elizabeth had seen nothing of such behavior. Mr. Darcy, she thought, was not a man to rattle along, speaking of nothing of substance like many a flirtatious young man with whom Elizabeth had been acquainted. One in particular, to her family's vast misfortune . . . .

Shaking off such thoughts, Elizabeth made some response to something Mr. Darcy said — though she could not say for certain either what he or she said — and returned to her thoughts of Mr. Darcy. While he did not make bland, banal conversation well, she thought, when it came to words of substance, he most certainly possessed considerable talent. He could speak of literature with little effort, his knowledge and experience extensive, his opinions intelligent, his insights often profound. It reminded Elizabeth greatly of the conversations she would often share with her father.

Her sadness at the thought of her father must have shown on her face, for Mr. Darcy paused and cast a concerned eye on her. "Are you cold, Miss Bennet? Shall we return to your uncle's home?"

"I am not cold," replied Elizabeth, smiling to reassure him. "It was nothing more than a stray thought."

It was difficult to determine if Mr. Darcy believed her, but he did not press the matter. To further distance herself from such thoughts, Elizabeth changed the subject.

"You should know that I am of a hardy constitution, Mr. Darcy. When I lived in the country, I walked nearly every day when the weather permitted it. The weather is still fine, though it is December. Were I still living in Hertfordshire, I would most assuredly have walked today."

"Walking is beneficial exercise," observed Mr. Darcy.

"It is. But I walk as much for the pleasure of nature as for the exercise."

"Then I hope to be in a position to show you Pemberley, my estate. The park is large — nearly twenty miles around — and much of it has been left to nature's sway, though there are formal gardens behind the house."

Feeling breathless at this new evidence of his growing regard, Elizabeth was silent for a moment. The accounts Georgiana gave her of her home, coupled with Mr. Darcy's words, however, made her curious. She could not help but ask:

"Can you tell me more of your home?"

Mr. Darcy smiled, informing Elizabeth that his home was one of his favorite subjects. "Pemberley is a jewel, Miss Bennet. I have the great fortune to call it my home. It is situated not far distant from the Peaks, close enough that on a clear day, from certain parts of the estate, one can see those majestic mountains rising in the distance.

"The estate itself is situated in a long valley surrounded by woods on three sides with a small river running through. In front of the house, the stream widens to form a small lake which provides me and my cousins many hours of amusement, fishing and swimming. It is the loveliest place in the world."

Bemused at his description—for a man who was not possessed of great powers of speech, Mr. Darcy had the soul of a poet!—Elizabeth could not help but question him further. "What do you produce on your estate?"

With a smile of true pleasure, Mr. Darcy began to recount the various industries in which his property participated. And it was in this recitation that Elizabeth began to truly understand his prominence in society. His estate was a small economy in its own right. While Elizabeth thought any man in possession of such an enterprise had a right to feel high and mighty, Mr. Darcy spoke of it with a certain level of pride, but more the pride of the work of his hands than any conceit.

They continued this way for some time, speaking softly about many subjects. It was not long, however, before they turned and began to make their way back toward the house. That was when Elizabeth was made uncomfortable again by a question posed by her companion.

"What of your home, Miss Bennet? Your father's estate must contain many beauties as well if your devotion to walking it is to be believed."

Confused for a moment, Elizabeth could not speak. Her silence was evident to her companion, who looked at her with pensive interest. The thought of explaining her recent past, coupled with the surety that he would turn away from her if he knew, prompted Elizabeth to respond quickly if only to keep his company a little longer.

"Longbourn is not a large estate, Mr. Darcy." She paused, knowing her dissembling would prick her conscience later, but unable to do anything else. "I believe I could walk from one end of the property to the other in perhaps two hours, though it is somewhat longer north to south. But it is pretty, with many groves of trees, ample fields of grain, and a low hill on the northern border which commands a fine view of the estate. I have climbed it often since I began walking as a girl."

"And what do you produce there?" asked Mr. Darcy.

Elizabeth gave him an account of the estate's enterprises, though she wondered if her information were still accurate. Given the current proprietor's abilities, she wondered if the estate suffered worse than it had under even her father's indifferent management.

"I am impressed, Miss Bennet."

His incongruous comment caught Elizabeth off guard. She peered at him, wondering as to his meaning.

"It is not often I have met a gentle young lady who knew anything of the activities which sustained her lifestyle," said Mr. Darcy, apparently understanding her confusion. "Georgiana is educated on the matter — she is my heir at present, and we Darcys have always felt it prudent that our daughters understand the importance of the estate. But many insipid young ladies of the ton are intent upon spending as much of their father's fortune as they can manage with nary a thought of how her ancestors amassed the wealth they enjoy."

"I am fully aware of the work that makes the estate function, Mr. Darcy. I have often helped my father with its operation, and have assisted with the tenants' concerns. It is not especially praiseworthy."

"Praiseworthiness is in the eye of the beholder, Miss Bennet," said Mr. Darcy. "From where I stand, praise is entirely due."

Elizabeth was saved from being required to respond by their return to her uncle's house. While Mrs. Gardiner invited Mr. Darcy to come in and enjoy tea with them, Mr. Darcy declined, citing an appointment. But Mrs. Gardiner was not finished with the gentleman.

"Then perhaps you and your dear sister would come to dinner one night this week. Would Thursday be convenient?"

"We would like that very much," said Mr. Darcy with evident pleasure.

Soon after, Mr. Darcy made his farewells and departed, leaving Elizabeth alone with her aunt. But while the elder woman regarded her with interest, Elizabeth was barely aware of it. Her mind was engaged in considering her recent days in the company of Mr. Darcy. And while her recollections were agreeable, the thought of speaking to him of matters best left forgotten cast a pall over her mind, forcing a measure of sadness into a situation which should contain nothing but joy.

"Here, Lizzy. This tea will do you some good."

Startled by the sound of her aunt's voice, Elizabeth reflexively took the cup her aunt was holding out to her. The tea had been delivered while she was caught in the grips of her own thoughts, and while Elizabeth was not of a mind to drink it, the scent was heavenly. She accepted the teacup and held it in her hand, allowing the heat of the liquid contained within to warm her hands. Her aunt sat nearby, sipping from her own cup, her eyes regarding Elizabeth from above the brim, calculating.

"It seems, Lizzy," said Mrs. Gardiner at length, when Elizabeth did not speak, "you have had an interesting time of late. Whoever would have thought you would come in contact with a man such as Mr. Darcy?"

"Not I," replied Elizabeth softly. Her aunt's words were too close to Elizabeth's thoughts for her to respond with her usual wit. The situation was such that Elizabeth was not certain how to act or what to do. She only knew that Mr. Darcy needed to know of her history before matters could continue any further.

"His inclination is very promising, is it not?" asked Mrs. Gardiner.

Elizabeth's eyes found her aunt's, considering the other woman's meaning. Knowing her relation, Mrs. Gardiner knew exactly what was troubling Elizabeth. No doubt she had considered the matter herself.

But Elizabeth felt disinclined to speak of it. It was personal, private — something she did not wish to discuss, even with her nearest and dearest relations. And yet, speaking of it would be cathartic, Elizabeth suspected, especially when she could count on the advice and support of her dearest aunt.

"I shall not press your confidence, Lizzy," said Mrs. Gardiner. "But I am willing to speak of it if you wish."

With those words, the dam was broken, and all Elizabeth's reticence fell away. She could no more have avoided speaking of it than she could have stopped the tide.

"I never dreamed I would be the subject of such ardent attentions," confided Elizabeth. "Especially since . . ."

Tears pricked the corners of her eyes, and she dashed them away angrily. "The best I could ever hope for is a marriage to a man of modest means, should I find one who will have me. As that possibility is not likely, a life of service, though it might be difficult to find an employer when they learn of my family's history."

"You know I do not agree with you on that score, Lizzy," reproved Mrs. Gardiner. "Mr. Darcy's attendance upon you these past days have amply demonstrated that, I should say."

"Mr. Darcy *is* a good man," replied Elizabeth. "The best of men. But he does not know. And I do not know how I can tell him, though I know it must be done."

"You do him a disservice."

Elizabeth laughed and shook her head. "Indeed, I do not. I could no more blame Mr. Darcy should he turn away from me than I could change the past. What man would not turn away from connecting himself to such a family as mine?"

"Lizzy," said Mrs. Gardiner, her tone stern. "One misstep is not the end of the world."

"That is not what society says."

"I am well aware of how society thinks. But I do not agree, nor do I believe you do. A person can only be responsible for their own actions, their own behavior. We have enough to worry about concerning our own lives to bother ourselves with the actions of others."

"No, Aunt, I do not agree with society." Elizabeth smiled, though it felt tremulous on her lips. "The relevant point, however, is not what you, I, or my uncle thinks. It is Mr. Darcy's opinion which must be of the utmost importance. He is a man of society. I cannot think he would want himself—his sister—connected with scandal and infamy."

"The matter is an old one, Lizzy. Furthermore, the gossip never left the neighborhood. Your family is not prominent enough to have their concerns disseminated with any interest in London."

"And yet, all it would take is for one whisper of it to be spoken. Then the matter would gain considerable interest, for I would not be an insignificant country miss any longer. I would be the wife of Mr. Darcy."

The act of actually saying it, giving words to her hopes, made Elizabeth shiver inside. It was not an exaggeration to suggest that she had given up all hope of ever making a good match—there had never been any *great* chance, not given her family's situation and her lack of dowry. But somehow, regardless of her endeavors to the contrary, her cynical outlook on life, the bitterness which had been a part of her life for so long she hardly remembered what it was like to be without it, she had allowed herself to hope.

And it was all so strange! Her acquaintance with Mr. Darcy was so brief that it could hardly be said that she even knew him. Elizabeth Bennet had always been a romantic young woman, and her parents' less than perfect union had instilled in her a desire to make a match based on mutual respect and love. But she had never believed in the phenomenon of falling in love on the basis of such a brief acquaintance. Love would come after respect, which would be built between two people after months of knowledge had been gained when the other person's character was well understood. In light of this, how could she have come to such a deep regard for Mr. Darcy? It had come on her suddenly, like a star shooting through the night sky, leaving a trail of light in its wake. It was incomprehensible.

"It seems to me, Lizzy," said her aunt, breaking the flow of Elizabeth's thoughts, "that you do not give your young man enough credit."

Elizabeth opened her mouth to protest, but Mrs. Gardiner held her hand up to silence her. "Mr. Darcy strikes me as a man who knows his mind, who would not be frightened away by a few whispers in the night. I suspect that he does not allow anything to get in the way of what he wants.

"I know you will likely protest that none of us know if he wants you."

Her mouth snapping shut, Elizabeth glared mutinously at her aunt, who only chuckled. Mrs. Gardiner reached out and patted Elizabeth's hand, before bringing her hand up to brush the back of her knuckles against Elizabeth's cheek. It was the affectionate gesture of a mother, causing tears to well up in Elizabeth's eyes. Mrs. Bennet was not the kind of woman to show spontaneous affection, and while Elizabeth's relationship with her mother had always been difficult, her knowledge of her mother's love did not extend to such displays.

"While I cannot claim to know Mr. Darcy's thoughts," continued Aunt Gardiner, "he shows all the symptoms of a man who admires a woman."

"He must be told," said Elizabeth quietly.

"Yes, that much is obvious. But I urge you not to expect the worst in his reaction, Lizzy. In the end, I suspect he will surprise you."

Mrs. Gardiner patted Elizabeth's knee and rose. "Now, I have some tasks I must complete. Why do you not spend some time resting in your room? It will do you good."

Then she departed, leaving Elizabeth to consider what she had said. In the end, the tepid cup of tea, which she still held in her hand, was consigned to the tray untouched, and Elizabeth took her aunt's advice. A short nap in her room would do her a world of good, and might actually allow her to consider matters more rationally.

While her nap did help settle Elizabeth's nerves, she did not find release in sleep, and it did not calm her to any great extent—at least with respect to Mr. Darcy and his attentions. In fact, while she found herself enjoying his company more by the day, her disquiet grew, for she knew what she must do, and she was not anticipating it in the slightest. It would be much more difficult to recover from the loss of a man with whom she had fallen in love than a good man with whom she had become good friends.

As soon as that thought occurred to her when she had retired to her room, the possibility of restful repose disappeared. For now, her thoughts were bent upon that ephemeral emotion, wondering if she loved Mr. Darcy. In the end, she concluded that she was not. But it was painfully evident that particular cliff was approaching rapidly, and it would require little effort for her to be pushed off into the abyss which lay beyond. Prudence, therefore, dictated she should take steps to protect what remained of her heart.

However, it has often been said that it is much easier to *determine* to do something than to actually do it. In the case of Elizabeth Bennet's growing admiration for Mr. Fitzwilliam Darcy, this proved to be especially true.

The next day was a Saturday, which meant she spent her day at the hospital. And thither went Mr. Darcy as well. While she did not wish to think on such things, Elizabeth's heart told her that he was matching his schedule to hers. Their interaction was limited but fraught with feelings which were new and wonderful to Elizabeth.

But the biggest threat to her equanimity occurred on Monday when she was again at the hospital. Elizabeth had found that she had many duties when at the hospital, and direct contact with the children was not always possible, though she often did keep them company, teaching them to read, helping them learn skills which would help them in life. In no way were her activities comparable to Mr. Darcy's, for his assistance was usually rendered in the larger matters of the hospital's management. On that day, however, Elizabeth noted that Mr. Darcy was engaged in a completely different activity.

"Please take these towels to Mrs. Potter," Elizabeth was instructed by the matron. Though carrying items from one location to another was not one of Elizabeth's favorite activities, but she set to it with a will. As she walked down toward where the linens were kept, she happened to pass by an open door, and the image which appeared as she glanced inside stopped her mid-stride.

"No, Jeremy. Hold the bat like this."

The sound of Mr. Darcy's voice floated out to her where he was standing with a group of the young boys, a cricket bat in the hand of the boy by his side, as he adjusted the lad's grip. The other boys all crowded around, trying to obtain a clear view of what the gentleman was showing their compatriot. As the boy became more comfortable with the grip and the weight of the bat, he began to take some experimental swings.

"Closer to the floor, " instructed Mr. Darcy, once again showing the young man the proper way to swing the bat. "The ball will come in low, and when you swing the bat, it should come in contact with the ball and hit it as far away as possible."

"And then you run to the base?" asked another of the boys.

"Are you skilled at this game?" demanded another.

Mr. Darcy laughed. "I am. Though I should not brag, no one could best me when I was at Cambridge."

A round of oohs and ahs met his statement, followed by further demands for their turns, which Mr. Darcy organized fairly and efficiently. As he concentrated on showing the boys what he knew, Elizabeth watched, spellbound, noting as he negotiated solutions to disputes, remonstrated eager young boys when necessary, and patiently assumed the role of both teacher and mentor. And given their interactions of the past few days, Elizabeth could not help but imagine these boys were *her* children, and that he was their father.

The thought caused Elizabeth's cheeks to suddenly burn as they never had before, and she took herself from that open door. But while she made her way to her destination, her heart and mind were not on her task. Instead, she was considering what she had seen, all she felt, and she knew this could not go on longer. Her communication must be made as soon as she could find the opportunity to do so. Further delay would only shatter her heart into an even greater jumble of pieces. It would not do.

The next day was the dinner to which Mr. and Miss Darcy had been invited, and while the setting was not one Elizabeth might have chosen, the urgency had settled in her heart. She wished it finished, the result to be decided upon, so she would not continue in this fashion. If he chose not to see her again after this, then so be it. At least she would know.

The sight of Mr. Darcy that evening brought painful palpitations to Elizabeth's heart. He was so tall and handsome in his blue coat, his hair curled at the edges of his collar, his eyes fixed upon her almost as soon as he entered the room. His sister by his side was similarly finely attired and appeared quite happy to see her, but Elizabeth had little attention to spare for Georgiana, though she attempted to act as she ever did.

They sat for a time, conversation flowing effortlessly between them. However, while Elizabeth could usually be found in the middle of such delights, that evening she found her mind too jumbled to join in. Mr. Darcy, she could see, watched her, his expression and air grave, as if he suspected what she wished to tell him. Knowing he was an intelligent man, Elizabeth suspected he had already guessed there were some difficulties in her past, though he could not know the particulars. While she was eager to relate to him all she knew, if only to end this exquisite torture, there was no opportunity to do so before they were called in to supper.

After the meal was a different story. The gentlemen, due to the small size of the party, declined to remain behind when the ladies retired to the sitting-room. There, in a move as cunning as any her mother might have engineered, Georgiana deliberately sat next to her aunt and uncle and engaged them in conversation, allowing Elizabeth to sit beside Mr. Darcy at a little distance from the rest of the company.

"Miss Bennet," said Mr. Darcy, "I do not believe I have had the opportunity to inform you how beautiful you appear tonight. I do not believe I have seen that dress you are wearing before. But it becomes you very well."

Suddenly self-conscious, Elizabeth glanced down at the pale green dress which she wore, and managed to respond, saying: "I often wear this dress when in company during the evenings."

"I can see why," was his soft reply.

"Mr. Darcy—" said Elizabeth, rushing to have her say before she lost her nerve.

But her sentence was never finished, for Mr. Darcy interrupted her. "It seems to me, Miss Bennet," said he, "that you have something, in particular, you wish to say to me. Might I assume it concerns the reason for your residence in your uncle's house?"

"It does," was Elizabeth's quiet reply.

"And might I assume you are afraid whatever you have to say will not reflect well on you?"

The recent days had seen enough blushes to last a lifetime, and Elizabeth felt her cheeks heat once again. But she managed a nod in his direction.

"Let me say first that there is nothing which could induce me to think less of you."

Elizabeth's eyes rose to meet his. There was an earnestness contained within them that warmed her through, like a sip of hot chocolate on a cold, wintery day. His surety somehow made her feel better, though she knew that he was likely devaluing what she had to say to him.

"If you would," said he, once again speaking before she could gather herself and make her lips form words, "perhaps we could defer this conversation until tomorrow? I would be more than happy to listen to whatever you deem it necessary that I understand. But tonight, in company with your aunt and uncle, and my sister, I would prefer to speak of happy thoughts. Is this acceptable?"

Perhaps it was the warmth in his tone, or it may have been the selfish desire to once again push the unpleasant duty to another time. Or perhaps she simply could deny this man nothing. Whatever it was, Elizabeth found herself agreeing. The rest of the evening was spent speaking of many things. And Elizabeth forgot about the troubling communication for a time.

CHAPTER V

*G*iven the ordeal which was to ensue that Wednesday, there was no question of going to the hospital. Not only was Elizabeth required to remain at her uncle's house to receive Mr. Darcy, but she would not have been in a position to concentrate on any task to which she was set. So she remained at home, alternately fidgeting and rising to pace about the room, nervous energy rolling off her in waves.

All of this Mrs. Gardiner watched with sympathy, though Elizabeth thought she detected more than a hint of amusement in her aunt's manner. Her aunt had been made aware of Elizabeth's plan to acquaint Mr. Darcy with the truth of the recent past. While she was supportive, she was nevertheless in disagreement with Elizabeth's opinion of the likely result of her communication.

"It is for the best, of course," said her aunt with a sigh. "I know you wish it were not required, Lizzy. But the sooner you dispense with it, the sooner it will cease to hang over your head like your own personal thundercloud."

Even that feeble jest failed to draw Elizabeth's attention, though under normal circumstances she might have teased her aunt for such a poor attempt at humor. Instead, she echoed her aunt's sigh.

"Well do I know it. I have felt . . ." Elizabeth trailed off, shook her head, and forced herself to continue. "It is obvious that Mr. Darcy is becoming attached to me, though I still can hardly fathom it."

"I can," was her aunt's soft reply.

Elizabeth shook her head. "Be that as it may, the communication must be made before matters progress too far. I would not have him learn of such things after he has taken an irreversible step."

"That is true."

Once again Elizabeth attempted to put a brave face on her approaching sorrow. "Once I have informed him of the truth, I can face whatever comes without no regrets."

Mrs. Gardiner regarded her with some affection before reaching up to touch and caress Elizabeth's cheek. "I know you expect him to turn away from you, Lizzy. But I have more faith in Mr. Darcy's fortitude. If he does refuse to see you anymore, I shall eat my bonnet."

Then with a laugh, Mrs. Gardiner forestalled a retort by saying: "I shall ensure you have a modicum of privacy with your young man. I will be in the next room, though you shall be required to leave the door open."

"Thank you, Aunt," said Elizabeth, unwilling to invite any further cheerful comments or teasing. She did not think they were warranted in this case, regardless of her aunt's opinion.

At the appointed time, Mr. Darcy presented himself to wait on them. As he walked into the room and greeted her, Elizabeth was struck once again with what a good man he was, how proper, precise, and careful he was. Mrs. Gardiner greeted him and engaged in some small conversation before departing. The door behind her as she left remained ajar as designed. Mr. Darcy did not even attempt to circumvent her authority, unlike some others Elizabeth might have suspected of trying the same measures.

"Miss Bennet," said Mr. Darcy, bowing over her hand. "How lovely it is to see you again."

"Mr. Darcy," replied Elizabeth softy. "Will you not sit?" She attempted a smile in his direction, though she could not have spoken for how convincing it was. "My aunt has allowed us this bit of privacy, so we may speak openly."

"That is kind of her," said Mr. Darcy. "Before we begin, however, I wished to ask for your opinion on a matter of some interest to us both."

This time Elizabeth felt her nervousness pierced by a hint of annoyance. It was as if the man was deliberately delaying the inevitable! But she assented, knowing it would more quickly take them to the reason for their meeting.

"Christmas is approaching, as you are aware," said Mr. Darcy, "and it is at this time of the year the children in the hospital suffer most for not having families of their own. I thought to hold a special gathering for them on Christmas day."

"That sounds wonderful, Mr. Darcy," said Elizabeth, her annoyance forgotten once again, washed away by the warmth she felt for the compassion of this man. "Perhaps we could have treats for the children, games, and Christmas carols? A visit from Father Christmas would also be special for them."

"Excellent!" said Mr. Darcy. "This was, in fact, Georgiana's notion, more than my own. Would it be acceptable if she were to speak with you about it, to plan what is needed? I can assure you the support of the governors for anything you wish to do."

"I would be happy to speak with Georgiana," replied Elizabeth, once again reminded of her purpose that day. Would Mr. Darcy still wish his sister to associate with her when he knew the truth? Only time would tell.

"Then perhaps we should move to the reason for my presence today," said Mr. Darcy. "First, I should explain my connection with Bingley and why we have become estranged, as I suspect my recital will be shorter and much less fraught with emotion than your own."

"That would be acceptable, Mr. Darcy," said Elizabeth, truly curious.

"If Bingley spoke of me," said Mr. Darcy, continuing, his manner speaking to his introspection, "you may have heard that we have been friends for several years."

"Yes," replied Elizabeth. "Mr. Bingley mentioned you had met at university and become good friends."

"That is true, though I will note that while we *did* meet at university, it was not until later that we became the firm friends we were for several years. I was in my last year at Cambridge when Bingley arrived for his first."

Mr. Darcy chuckled and shook his head. "Bingley was, you see, perhaps the greenest man I have ever met. He was lost at university, and while he is intelligent and would likely have learned what he needed to know quickly, I was drawn to him immediately and took him under my wing. By the end of that year, we had become firm friends, and while we parted at the end of the year and did not meet again for two years after, we did keep in contact, after a fashion, through correspondence."

"That must have been a chore, Mr. Darcy," said Elizabeth. "I have seen examples of Mr. Bingley's hand. It is truly atrocious."

The grin lighting Mr. Darcy's face became him. "It is due to those years of correspondence that I acquired the skill of deciphering his handwriting. But it was difficult at first." The grin faded from Mr. Darcy's face, and he became somber. "Soon after I left Cambridge, my father passed suddenly, leaving me with Georgiana's guardianship and an estate to manage. Those two years were necessary for me to learn what I needed to know to ensure my family's legacy.

"It was soon after I encountered Bingley again that I met his sister."

Elizabeth smirked and nodded at the gentleman. "Somehow I suspected this tale would include the lady at some point."

"I had not made the lady's acquaintance for more than five minutes before she decided she would be the next mistress of my home. I endured her for the sake of Bingley's friendship for the next few years, but privately I informed him I would never offer for her, nor marry her should she choose a more . . . direct method of obtaining that which she wanted."

"Did she, Mr. Darcy?" asked Elizabeth. "I never would have suspected her of being that lost to everything proper, but now I am not sure."

"She did not, thankfully." The gentleman paused, again deep in thought. "Perhaps she knew I would never put up with it, though that is attributing a level of sagacity to her I am not sure she ever possessed.

"Two summers ago, in early June, Bingley, Miss Bingley, and the Hursts visited Pemberley. And while I could endure Miss Bingley's attentions to me, her behavior in my home was everything objectionable. You may not credit it, Miss Bennet, but the longer she was in residence, the more she attempted to act as the estate's mistress."

"Oh, I do believe it, Mr. Darcy."

Mr. Darcy snorted with disdain. "I am sure you do. In the end, my housekeeper came to me, reporting that Miss Bingley had attempted to usurp certain functions of the house which are the purview of the mistress. Her pursuit of me was tolerable. But I could not allow her to embarrass my sister in her own home. And she was but fifteen at the time!"

"Though I attempted to deal with the matter with Miss Bingley to spare her from embarrassment, she denied everything and even demanded I replace my housekeeper, a woman of extensive experience who has been a family retainer all her life. Thus, I took the matter to Bingley."

Mr. Darcy grimaced. "You are familiar with Bingley, Miss Bennet. His temperament is inviting, but it is also his undoing with respect to his sister. He dislikes confrontation of any kind and declined to censure her. I told them I would not tolerate Miss Bingley's behavior any longer, and the visit ended abruptly soon thereafter. The last time I spoke to Bingley, I advised him that unless he took his sister in hand, she would be the ruin of him in society."

"It is less than I expected, Mr. Darcy," said Elizabeth. "But you acted properly in every respect. The fault lies with Miss Bingley." Elizabeth smiled at him. "You may find that Mr. Bingley is of a firmer character now, should you re-establish contact with him. He withstood all Miss Bingley's displeasure and married my sister, after all. Miss Bingley was not shy about stating her opinion within our hearing, I assure you."

A shaken head was Mr. Darcy's response, his lips had thinned in the memory of his vexation. "Miss Bingley has always sought to rise above her origins, which is what prompted her behavior toward me. She undoubtedly would have considered her brother's marriage to anyone other than an heiress from a wealthy and respected family to be a blow to her ambitions."

"No doubt," replied Elizabeth softly, sensing the moment of her own confession had begun.

Mr. Darcy peered at her for a moment, making her feel quite uncomfortable by his scrutiny. Then he gestured to her, and in a tender voice, said: "That is the extent of my connection with Bingley. Now, I believe you have something to say to me?"

"I do." Elizabeth's voice was small, timid, but she had no power to inject anything more into it.

"In a strange manner, my family's troubles seem almost connected with your estrangement with Mr. Bingley, for they began only a few months after. I do not know how much you are aware of Mr. Bingley's movements, but it was last year about Michaelmas when he first came to Hertfordshire. He leased the neighboring estate to my father's, and we became acquainted with him at an assembly soon after."

A slow nod was Mr. Darcy's reply. "I recall he was to lease an estate. We had spoken of it during Bingley's stay at Pemberley, and he had mentioned there was a property in Hertfordshire which had caught his eye. I had intended to attend him at his estate to help him learn to manage it, but our falling out rendered that impossible."

For a briefest of moments, Elizabeth wondered what might have happened had Mr. Darcy appeared at Netherfield with Mr. Bingley. If she had met him last autumn, would she have fallen in love with him as quickly as she had? Or would something have happened to come between them? Surely her family would have chased him away. Or perhaps she might have been married to him when her world fell apart, and she would be happy, instead of expecting him to pull away. Then again, it was better this way, for he might have resented her for bringing scandal to his family.

"Mr. Bingley did lease Netherfield, and he soon made himself agreeable to all the neighborhood. A particular recipient of his attentions was my elder sister, Jane." Elizabeth smiled at the memory of Jane's happiness the previous year. "As you already know, Mr. Bingley and Jane were married in February, to their great joy and his sister's chagrin."

"I can well imagine it, Miss Bennet," said Mr. Darcy. "Miss Bingley is disdainful of everyone she meets whom she considers not worth her time." He paused and laughed. "On the other hand, she is almost servile when confronted by those she wishes to impress. It is an interesting dichotomy, indeed."

"Miss Bingley would not be the first I have met who displays such disparate qualities," said Elizabeth dryly. "Regardless, she is not truly germane to the conversation." A thought entered Elizabeth's mind, and she stilled a little, before murmuring: "At least, not yet."

While she thought Mr. Darcy might interject, the gentleman held his peace and allowed her to gather her thoughts. After a moment, and in a stronger voice, Elizabeth was finally able to continue.

"At approximately the same time, two other gentlemen came to the area, and they are both also important to my tale, though one only peripherally. The first was my father's cousin, the parson of a living in Kent. And, perhaps, the most ridiculous man to whom I have ever been introduced."

"That is a grand statement, Miss Bennet," said Mr. Darcy, his eyes twinkling with interest and humor. "Silliness is all around us, after all. In fact, I dare say it is an epidemic of prodigious proportions."

"Indeed, you are correct, sir. But should you ever be introduced to my father's cousin, you would certainly agree. He is tall, heavyset, in possession of a strange mixture of pomposity and servility, and has not had an original thought enter his head which has not originated from his patroness, a woman of some property, I believe. My father and my cousin's father had long been estranged, and it was at her urging that he came to heal the breach in the families, instructing him to find a wife from amongst my father's daughters."

Mr. Darcy's eyes grew wide, and he regarded Elizabeth with something akin to astonishment. "I am sorry, Miss Bennet, but this recital has caused me to recall an acquaintance I made last spring. Your cousin would not, by any chance, be Mr. Collins of Hunsford?"

Astonished did not begin to describe Elizabeth's response. "You *know* Mr. Collins?"

"Not to any great degree," said Mr. Darcy. "I retract my earlier statement — Mr. Collins is quite as ridiculous as you suggest. But what you are not aware of is that my aunt, Lady Catherine de Bourgh, is Mr. Collins's patroness."

Elizabeth colored, her surprise turning to shame. It was not enough she was about to drive Mr. Darcy away due to the behavior of her improper family, but she had to insult his aunt.

"Do not concern yourself, Miss Bennet," said Mr. Darcy. "I shall not go into details now, but I am estranged from my aunt at present. You could not say anything of her which I have not already thought."

"But this is a curious coincidence, Mr. Darcy," said Elizabeth.

"It is, indeed. But I believe you were about to tell me what Mr. Collins has to do with your tale, though I believe I can guess."

"No doubt you can," replied Elizabeth with a grimace. "I was the fortunate recipient of Mr. Collins's addresses. Obviously, I refused him, was supported by my father, and that was the end of the matter. Mr. Collins married my close friend, Charlotte Lucas, and returned to Kent with her."

"Mrs. Collins struck me as a lady of some intelligence," said Mr. Darcy.

Elizabeth nodded but did not trust herself to speak on the matter again. "My mother, unfortunately, was not sanguine about the lost opportunity. Mr. Collins was my father's heir due to an entailment, and as my sisters and I have not much fortune among us, my mother was always frantic about the entail." Elizabeth paused, throwing a pleading look at him. "I hope you do not think me selfish, Mr. Darcy. I understood our circumstances, but I could not marry such a foolish man as Mr. Collins. Misery would have been my constant companion in such a union."

"Some might censure you," said Mr. Darcy, his compassion overflowing in his voice. "But I am not one of them. Witness to my parents' close union of admiration and respect as I was, I understand the need for such sentiments in a marriage."

"Something my parents never enjoyed," whispered Elizabeth. "That is the primary reason why I vowed never to marry for anything less than love."

It was incongruous, Elizabeth decided, to feel such relief at his continued good opinion. The next part of her account would no doubt destroy it forever.

"The other man who came to Hertfordshire during this time had a much more damaging effect on my family. A company of militia was wintering in Meryton, and to their number was added another, a snake who wore the mantle of a man of charm and goodness. But there was nothing good about Mr. Wickham."

This time Mr. Darcy's eyes fairly bulged out of his head, and he gaped at her. "Mr. Wickham?" demanded he. "Mr. George Wickham?"

Bewildered, Elizabeth could only nod. Mr. Darcy nodded once.

"Though it seems improbable at best, I am also acquainted with Mr. Wickham, Miss Bennet. I am probably more familiar with his character than you could ever be."

Elizabeth was all perplexity. "You know Mr. Wickham?"

With a nod and a sigh, Mr. Darcy explained: "He is the son of my father's steward. My connection with him has long been dissolved, and I will not distress you by giving you an account of his proclivities or his offenses against my family." Mr. Darcy paused and grimace. "Would that I had not fallen out with Bingley. If I had not, I might have been in a position to offer some protection to your family."

"My family should have been in a position to defend its own interests," said Elizabeth, dashing her tears away. The old anger had been rekindled, forcing her to fight it off lest it overwhelm her. After a moment she continued her tale dully, wishing this mortifying interview to be over as soon as possible.

"There are a few more things you should know of my family, Mr. Darcy. My mother was not born a gentlewoman, nor is she possessed of much sense, and my father, while an intelligent man, found himself worn down by years of her nerves, often retreating to his library to avoid her, and thereby, avoid his responsibilities to the family. In particular, though Jane and I had largely been influenced by the Gardiners, and my middle sister is of a disposition which did not lend itself to misbehavior, my youngest two sisters are silly and vain, neither possessing much sense. Especially Lydia, my youngest sister. In her, Mr. Wickham found an easy target."

Mr. Darcy closed his eyes in seeming regret. When he opened them again, they were filled with pain, but intent upon her. When he spoke again, Elizabeth was surprised by the gentle tone he used, though it was infused with a command.

"Tell me, Miss Bennet."

With a shrug, Elizabeth turned her head away. "I am sure you know enough of him to guess, Mr. Darcy. He persuaded my foolish sister to acts which no lady can commit and remain a gentlewoman. My father, to his credit, was incensed when he discovered the matter and called Wickham out. He never returned from that meeting, for Wickham killed him."

A gasp escaped Mr. Darcy's lips. "Wickham? He was *never* violent, though all manner of other vices may be attributed to him."

"He claimed it was an accident," said Elizabeth, the pain in her head and heart threatening to overwhelm her. "Regardless, my father was shot through the heart, and Wickham was prosecuted and hanged. My sisters and I were ruined, and Mr. Collins took a great deal of pleasure in turning us out of our home."

"What became of your mother and sisters?"

"Mr. Bingley had already been married to Jane for some months by then. He took his responsibilities seriously, and with my uncle's assistance, let a cottage for them in a neighboring shire. But then, fearing the taint of scandal, he severed all contact and moved his small family to York to escape it. I shall never forget the look of utter contempt and loathing Miss Bingley bestowed upon us the last time I saw her."

"And why are you not with them now?"

Elizabeth looked up wanly at Mr. Darcy. It was heartening to see that he regarded her with compassion, rather than the contempt she had almost expected to see. Not that it would do her any good. Surely any good man, sensible of a younger sister and his position in society, would flee from her now.

"My mother, as you can imagine, railed at me in particular for my refusal of Mr. Collins. The situation was so . . . uncomfortable that I applied to my uncle for support, and I came to London not long after."

"And Miss Lydia?"

Anger once again took hold of Elizabeth's heart. "The stupid, silly girl actually blamed our father for her disgrace and wailed about how she would have been married to Mr. Wickham, had our father not interfered. She disappeared from Longbourn even before my mother was removed to the cottage, and we have not seen her since." Elizabeth snorted with disgust. "It is likely for the best, as her disgrace did not follow my family to our new lodgings."

Returning to her contemplation of her hands, Elizabeth could only whisper: "The worst part of it has been the separation from Jane. She has always been my closest friend and confidante. I miss her very much."

With those words, Elizabeth fell silent, feeling drained of all emotion now that her confession had been made. Outside the window, a bird chirped and sang its song of joy, insensible to the storm of emotion which had been released inside. For a brief moment, Elizabeth considered it, wondering at the freedom being a bird must bring, wondering if sorrow were an incomprehensible concept to a bird. She could not help but chuckle softly to herself at such inane thoughts. She was becoming as senseless as Lydia.

At her side, Mr. Darcy shifted slightly, no more than a slight move to a different sitting position. But Elizabeth, who was now sensitive to everything the man did, noted it and wondered if it presaged his immediate departure. She could not blame him—she had never thought to blame him. He was the best man of her acquaintance, a man who, in other circumstances, would have fit all her wishes in a marriage partner. Lydia's disgrace destroyed all that.

"When did this all happen, Miss Bennet?" asked Mr. Darcy at length.

Still unable to look up at him, Elizabeth shrugged. "Mr. Collins arrived in November, Mr. Wickham only a day or two later. My sister was married in January. Lydia's disgrace happened in April, and the remainder of my family was removed to Essex soon after. Mr. Collins was not slow in asserting his rights to my father's estate, I assure you."

"It would have been soon after my visit to Kent," said Mr. Darcy. "You have not seen any of your family since coming away?"

Moved by the compassion in his voice, Elizabeth finally looked up. He appeared more than a little distracted. Elizabeth understood—her power over him was sinking beneath the weight of what she had revealed.

"I have not. I do receive letters from Mary and Kitty, my sisters remaining with my mother." Once again Elizabeth mustered a smile. "It seems their new residence has been good for them both. They have learned to rely on each other. Mr. Bingley and my uncle provide their support, but as their circumstances are much diminished, they do not live the way they might previously have expected. At least the scandal has not followed them to their new home."

Mr. Darcy nodded. "Yours is a sad tale, Miss Bennet. I am grieved, indeed, you have had to endure it."

"Thank you, sir."

"I would remind you also that it is often said it is darkest before the dawn." Mr. Darcy looked at her, the intensity in his gaze causing her to shiver, though she knew not why. "You have not allowed this tragedy to destroy you, and you are to be commended for it."

"I do not believe I have done anything extraordinary, Mr. Darcy."

"Perhaps not," said he with a smile of encouragement. "But you have withstood the storms of life, and that requires some fortitude. It is clear that is one quality you have in abundance.

They spoke for some few more minutes. Mr. Darcy was kind and supportive, raising her spirits ever so slightly with his continued attention. But it was also clear that he was distracted, and given the weight of what she had just related, she knew exactly of what he was thinking. It did not bode well for their future association.

At length, Mr. Darcy indicated his need to depart. He did so by rising and bowing over her hand, saying: "I shall see you anon, Miss Bennet. At present, there are matters to which I must attend, and I believe some rest would do you good. Until next time."

With those final words, he took his leave. Elizabeth watched him go, thinking it likely she would never see him again, despite his words to the contrary.

CHAPTER VI

"*M*iss Bennet?"

Elizabeth blinked, startled from her thoughts. The sea of young, cherubic faces met her eyes, most puzzled or concerned.

A blush made its way up her cheeks, and she hung her head. The book she had been reading to the young girls of the hospital sat forgotten in her hands. The realization that she had become distracted in the middle of reading it settled over her, and she felt all that much more embarrassed at her inability to remain focused on her task.

"Is something wrong, Miss Bennet?" asked one of the girls. She was the eldest of the group, though one of the smallest. Her name was Genevieve, and she was by far the most vocal.

"No, Genevieve," said Elizabeth, favoring the girl with a smile. "All is well. I am afraid I became distracted by a random thought."

It was clear the girl did not believe her. "Mrs. Mason often tells us we must rely on each other. Shall you not tell us your troubles, so we may help you?"

The other girls chorused their approval, gathering around Elizabeth, entreating her to share her regrets with them. Elizabeth's heart was full at the sight of these girls, alone in the world, left to shift for themselves, turning their attention on her for her benefit. In a world where it often seemed there was much strife and grief and very little charity, Elizabeth was moved by their interest. But she would not share her recent problems with anyone, for they were far too personal.

"Mrs. Mason is a very wise woman," said Elizabeth of the matron of the Foundling Hospital. "You do well to listen to her. And how can anyone be unhappy when with all of you? I find myself very blessed, indeed.

"Now, let us continue reading."

The girls settled again to listen to Elizabeth, though several still looked at her with questioning gazes. Elizabeth ignored them, however; this time focusing on the book in her hands, determined not to allow her troubled thoughts to control her again. In time, the book was completed, and Elizabeth seated the children at the nearby table, providing them with charcoal and paper, where they could practice their letters. Reading and writing was a skill which would help them make their way in the world, and Elizabeth was gratified the directors at the hospital recognized this fact, ensuring they were taught these skills which would be so useful in life.

As she made her way around the tables, assisting where necessary, explaining in a gentle fashion where required, her thoughts once again slipped back to the recent past, including her confession to Mr. Darcy the previous day. Thursday was not her usual day to attend the children at the hospital. But the conversation had affected her equilibrium to the extent that she was wild for a distraction and had petitioned her uncle to be allowed to go to the hospital that day. Mr. Gardiner, knowing his niece, had given her his affectionate permission, making sure his repaired carriage was at her disposal.

Though Elizabeth did not know which days Mr. Darcy made himself available to the hospital, he was not there that day, a matter which disheartened Elizabeth even further. Had he decided that he would now avoid her at all costs? His words the previous day had been encouraging, but she had not expected him to openly censure her. The fact that he could not know she intended to be there that day she thought of, but she knew he would have the means at his disposal to know if she were present if he wished.

It had been far more painful than Elizabeth had ever expected. The shame of relating her family's history had been bad enough. Laying it bare to a man she respected, a man who filled all her hopes in a future companion, was sheer torture. If they remained friends, if he never made his addresses to her for whatever reason, Elizabeth could have lived with it. To know he was in the world thinking ill of her, relieved at his escape, was more than Elizabeth could bear.

"Miss Bennet! Miss Bennet!"

Elizabeth approached Genevieve, who was beckoning to her, looking down at the paper in front of her. "Did I do it right?" asked she in an excited tone.

On the paper, the girl had written her own name, in letters neat and concise. Elizabeth was about to compliment her on her skill when she looked a little further down and saw her own name, spelled with two I's, with Mr. Darcy's name on the same line. Then below it, Genevieve had written her own name, along with Elizabeth's, with the surname of Darcy.

Again embarrassed beyond measure, Elizabeth gazed at the page, seeing her own name for the first time with Mr. Darcy's surname, and she knew she was in love with the gentleman.

Somehow, she managed to restrain the tears from spilling from her eyes as she gazed at the page, unable to look away. By her side, Genevieve looked up at her with concern, the smile turning into a frown, and then to sadness, accompanied by the trembling of her lower lip. It was the girl's distress which pulled Elizabeth away from her own feelings to provide comfort.

"Your writing is very fine," said Elizabeth, forcing the stab of sorrow away. She enveloped the girl in an embrace. "I am pleased with how quickly you have learned."

Sensing Elizabeth was not upset with her, Genevieve calmed and looked up at her with trusting eyes. "I am sorry, Miss Bennet. I should not have put Mr. Darcy's name with mine. It is just . . ."

"I know, dear heart," said Elizabeth. "It is difficult being alone in the world, and you wish for a family. It is understandable."

"Do you have a family, Miss Bennet?"

"I do," replied Elizabeth. "I live with my aunt and uncle, and my mother and two sisters live in Essex." Elizabeth could not talk about Jane—it was still too painful.

Genevieve looked up at her with some curiosity. "I think you should marry Mr. Darcy."

Shocked, Elizabeth returned the girl's earnest gaze. "What would make you say such a thing?"

"I have seen him looking at you," said the girl amid a giggle. "I wish a man would look at me like that. I wish Mr. Darcy were *my* father and you were my mother. I would be so happy!"

"I have no doubt you would be," replied Elizabeth gently. "You will not always live here, Genevieve. Learn everything you can, and when you go out into the world, I am sure you will find a man who will love you."

With a beaming smile, Genevieve turned back to her paper and began to practice her letters again, leaving Elizabeth watching her with bemusement. One thing she had learned quickly when coming to the hospital was the hopes and dreams of the children. It was not surprising they would wish for a family, dream of loving parents, a home in which they would be allowed to grow and thrive. To have a future.

But never before had Elizabeth heard one of these children speak of such specific wishes, particularly involving her and Mr. Darcy. The thought of the gentleman once again brought a tenderness to Elizabeth's breast, and for the moment at least, her sorrow receded to the back of her mind. Regardless of Mr. Darcy's retreat, she would always possess the warmest feelings for the gentleman. He had brought her some measure of happiness in a dark time. He was simply the best man of her acquaintance.

In a part of town, far removed from the Foundling Hospital, a young gentleman sat in his study, pondering the events of the past days. The more he thought, the more Fitzwilliam Darcy did not like his own conduct.

It was a truth in society that those who possessed wealth and standing also possessed a certain amount of power. While the Darcy family had never been of the peerage, they had always possessed a certain prestige, not only because of the wealth which had been built by centuries of his family's forebears but also because of their reputation and connections to those of higher society. His uncle was a good example of Darcy connections to earls, though not the only one.

In fact, Darcy was troubled by Miss Bennet's account, and more particularly because he knew it had been in his power to prevent it from ever happening. Darcy had always known what Wickham was, from the days when they had been young men together. Wickham had displayed characteristics which branded him a libertine and a womanizer, among other vices, as young as thirteen or fourteen years of age.

But Darcy had refrained from informing his father of Wickham's base character, preferring, instead, to distance himself, to blunt the effects of Wickham's excesses in his own way. Had he told his father, would Wickham have been forced to change or be cast off? Darcy had no answer to that question. At the very least, after years of paying his debts and compensating him for the family living, when Wickham had betrayed him by trying to seduce Georgiana, Darcy knew he should have taken action. While his intention of protecting Georgiana's reputation was laudable, Darcy possessed the power to have Wickham quietly transported, and if he did not, his uncle, the earl, certainly did.

His decision to allow Wickham to go free yet again had no doubt caused heartache for not only the Bennet family but also for many others Wickham assuredly defrauded before he finally met his fate. That Wickham was now gone was a matter of surprise to Darcy. He had quietly had the man watched for years and had continued that practice after his attempt with Georgiana. Once it became clear that Wickham would not speak of what happened, Darcy had decided to relax his watch, as he wanted nothing more to do with his former friend. It appeared that was a miscalculation as well.

Regret was one thing. But Darcy knew that to truly atone for his mistakes, he needed to attempt to make the situation right—or as right as he could. And it was for this reason he was ensconced in his study, trying to decide how he might go about doing it. That was where Georgiana found him that morning.

"You have been in here all morning, Brother," said his sister by way of greeting. "I hope all is well with Miss Bennet? Usually, you would be visiting her at this hour."

Darcy gazed at his sister fondly. It was a blessing that she had taken to Miss Bennet so quickly. A shy soul at heart, Georgiana had always found it difficult to speak with others, a trait which had not been present in Miss Bennet's company since their first meeting in the carriage. That it also boded well for Darcy's future hopes was not something he had neglected to consider.

"There is nothing the matter with Miss Bennet," said Darcy. "I have merely been considering what she told me when I visited her yesterday." Darcy sighed and leaned against his hand, staring moodily at the fire across the room. "Miss Bennet has suffered, Georgiana. And I cannot help but acknowledge that some of the blame is mine to bear."

A frown met his declaration. "How could you possibly bear any blame for whatever trials Miss Bennet has borne?"

Cursing himself for a fool, Darcy paused, unsure what he should tell his sister. Georgiana was quite recovered from her experience with George Wickham, but he was wary of reopening old wounds.

"You are quite frightening me, Brother," said Georgiana. Her tone was light, but the underlying concern existed in her voice. "Please share it with me. I wish to help."

"I cannot say much," replied Darcy, "for Miss Bennet has not authorized me to speak of it. But I can inform you that it involves a certain *gentleman* of our acquaintance, an unfortunate acquaintance, to be sure."

For a moment, Georgiana did not appear to understand his reference. Then her face lit up with comprehension, and she gaped at him. "Are you suggesting Miss Bennet's troubles have been caused by Mr. Wickham?"

"To a large extent, yes," said Darcy. He favored his sister with a rueful smile. "That is not all. Miss Bennet's cousin was once Lady Catherine's parson. Add her eldest sister's marriage to Bingley, and we have far more connections to the Bennet family than I could have imagined."

Georgiana, still apparently shocked to hear Wickham's name again, did not immediately reply. At length, however, she gathered her wits about her and said in a soft voice: "That is curious, indeed. I suppose I shall have to beg Elizabeth for an accounting of what has happened. If Mr. Wickham was involved, I know it cannot be good."

Darcy peered at his sister curiously. "I was reluctant to mention his name in your presence."

"I am much recovered from my experience with Mr. Wickham," said Georgiana impatiently. "My concern is much more for Elizabeth." A look of horror came over her face. "He—he did not importune her improperly, did he?"

"Not Miss Bennet, no," replied Darcy. "For anything else, you will have to ask her. I apologize, Georgiana, but I cannot betray her confidence. Suffice to say that Wickham wreaked havoc on the Bennet family, as he has on others in many other occasions."

Darcy paused, equally uncertain if he should bring up this next point. When he spoke, it was hesitantly. "Of George Wickham, you may set yourself at ease. Among Miss Bennet's communications was the fact that he has finally paid for his actions."

A gasp escaped Georgiana's lips. "Are you referring to his demise?"

With a nod, Darcy added: "He was apparently hanged for his actions with respect to the Bennet family. Though I cannot but sorrow for a life wasted, I cannot say he was not on this path for many years. I have no doubt our father has already made his displeasure known to Wickham."

"I have no doubt Papa was looking down on him with disgust. I cannot imagine he would have been greeted with anything less."

While Darcy agreed with her, he suspected his father was watching Darcy himself with less than true pleasure. Once again Darcy's mind turned to thoughts of his own failures concerning Wickham. Georgiana seemed to see this, for she looked at him askance.

"What is it, William?"

Darcy sighed and passed a hand over his brow. "I have only been thinking of my own culpability in the matter of Mr. Wickham."

"How can you possibly be to blame for Mr. Wickham's misdeeds?"

"For his deeds, I can bear no blame—at least when we were younger. But I knew what Wickham was for many years. Not only did I not speak to our father on the subject, but I also did nothing to curb his excesses. At the very least, I should have done something when he attempted to secure you and your dowry."

Georgiana paused and thought for several minutes before she fixed him with a sympathetic gaze. "Perhaps there is some truth in what you say. But Mr. Wickham was his own man and made his own decisions. I am well aware that what you did after Ramsgate was for my protection, and for that I am grateful. Do not allow Mr. Wickham to have such power over you, even after he is gone. He made his own choices."

While Darcy still felt the burden of his own actions, in some small way, Georgiana's words made him feel lighter, as if a weight had been removed from his shoulders. Standing, Darcy made his way around the desk, drew his sister to her feet, and enveloped her in a fierce embrace. Georgiana returned his gesture with her own brand of fervor, and they stood for some moments, drinking in the comfort of the other.

"I wish our cousin were here," Darcy said at last. "He is always able to pull us from our dourness and make us laugh."

His words caused Georgiana to respond in exactly the same way their favorite cousin would have. Then she sobered.

"I hope he is well."

"He is a member of the general staff and should be well clear of any fighting," said Darcy. "I have no doubt he will return in due time to bedevil us all over again."

Georgiana laughed and drew away. "May I visit Elizabeth tomorrow, Brother? If her experiences with Mr. Wickham have been as difficult as you suggest, I wish to sympathize with her."

Regarding her curiously, Darcy said: "Do you mean to tell her about Ramsgate?"

A half-hearted shrug was her response. "Perhaps, though I have made no determination as of yet. I do wish to hear of her troubles, though, and to be a friend to her."

"A better friend she could not find," said Darcy warmly.

Gesturing back to her chair, Darcy took one nearby and fixed an intent gaze upon her. "It is my thought that I should like to do what I can to make amends for my lack of action concerning Wickham. While I cannot undo everything he has done, I wish to do whatever I can."

"You love her, do you not?"

Georgiana's sudden question hung between them and Darcy, uncomfortable with speaking of his feelings, remained silent for a moment. But he could not deny it — not to himself, and not to his dear sister.

"We have not been acquainted for long. But already I feel a powerful connection with her. I do not know what will come of it, but I do know I wish for her presence in my life."

Gleefully, Georgiana clapped her hands, exclaiming: "I knew it! Now I shall have the sister I always wished to have!"

"Let us not put the cart before the horse, Georgiana," said Darcy, laughing at her enthusiasm. "Before anything can be between us, I must fix some of the trouble Wickham has caused."

"How do you mean to do that?"

"I have a few ideas." Darcy paused, thinking of the possibilities he had considered before. "There are several things which would make her happy. There are a few, in particular, I would like to pursue."

"I will assist in any way I can."

Darcy smiled at his sister, reached for her hand, and squeezed it in thanks. "The first thought I had was concerning Bingley. As you know, we have been estranged for a time. I had thought to make some overtures to heal the breach between us."

"Is Mr. Bingley not married to Elizabeth's sister?"

"She is," confirmed Darcy. "Being reunited with her sister would surely bring Miss Bennet joy. And I should enjoy having Bingley's company again."

"What of Miss Bingley?" asked Georgiana.

Darcy frowned. "I suppose I might consider admitting her back into my society, little though I wish for it. Miss Bingley will not be invited to Pemberley again, regardless of the status of my friendship with her brother. I suppose, in light of that fact, there is little to be gained from continuing to shun her."

"And you will gain further protection from her should you marry."

Georgiana's sly comment prompted Darcy to laugh delightedly. "Perhaps that is so. If it is, I shall be very grateful, indeed, to be spared the threat of the most fearsome predator I have ever encountered."

They laughed together and continued to speak together for some time. While nothing was settled, Darcy began to feel better about the situation. Nothing could be done about certain parts of Miss Bennet's tale, for Wickham's depravity had stolen those possibilities away from them all. But much could still be done. And whatever could be accomplished, Darcy was determined to do it.

CHAPTER VII

To Elizabeth's great surprise, the following day saw a visitor to Gracechurch Street she had not expected to see again. Mrs. Gardiner insisted she was wrong in her suppositions, but Elizabeth, perhaps showing the stubbornness for which most the Bennet family had long been renowned, would not heed her. Thus, to see Miss Georgiana Darcy enter the room, announced by the housekeeper, was a shock.

"Mrs. Gardiner, Miss Bennet," said Miss Darcy, curtseying prettily. "How do you do this morning?"

Finding herself bereft of words, Elizabeth could only stare in response to the girl's greeting. Mrs. Gardiner, however, found herself completely equal to the task, but not before she shot a smug glance in Elizabeth's direction.

"We are completely well, Miss Darcy. I hope your brother is also well? We have missed his company."

"William is well. He has been busy with some business of late, but I should not be surprised if he were to call on you in the near future."

Taking a seat at Mrs. Gardiner's request, Georgiana sat to visit with them while her aunt called for a tea service. The shock which Elizabeth felt upon seeing her quickly turned to curiosity, for while Georgiana spoke in a friendly manner, her frequent glances at Elizabeth spoke of a reason for her visit quite beyond a simple social call. Elizabeth was intrigued, for such behavior was not what she would have expected. Surely her brother must have informed her of the disgrace of Elizabeth's family.

When they had continued in the manner for some time in banal conversation, Georgiana changed the subject abruptly. "Mrs. Gardiner, I know the length of a normal visit, but I would ask your indulgence this morning, for I have something particular of which I wish to speak with your niece. Might I request some time for a private conversation with Miss Bennet?"

By now, Elizabeth felt her eyebrows disappearing into her hairline. While Georgiana had become much more accustomed to her friendship, enough to be comfortable in her company, she was still a gentle, unassuming girl, little inclined to put herself forward. In this instance, she appeared more like her brother, who Elizabeth had always known was a self-possessed man.

For her aunt's part, she seemed bemused by the request, though not at all disinclined to grant it. She snuck a look, carrying a wealth of meaning, in Elizabeth's direction, before she turned to Georgiana with a smile.

"Miss Darcy," said she, her voice slightly chiding, "I believe there is no need for such formality between us. You may come and visit at any time, and we are happy to host you here as long as you wish to stay. Speak with Lizzy as long as you wish. If you are still here when the time arrives for luncheon, we would be happy to have you stay and partake with us."

Georgiana beamed and thanked Mrs. Gardiner, who then excused herself to allow them to speak privately. Though curious of Georgiana's purpose, Elizabeth could not help but feel more than a hint of trepidation at the same time. This new, forceful emergence of Georgiana's character could be provoked by no reason other than to warn Elizabeth away from her brother.

Such thoughts, however, were immediately dispelled by Georgiana's next action. Rising from her seat, Georgiana approached her position on the sofa and sat by her side, her hands reaching for Elizabeth's grasping them tightly.

"Elizabeth," said she, her countenance entirely serious, "I spoke with my brother yesterday, and while he would not inform me of the subject of your conversation, he gave me to understand you have experienced hardship at the hands of Mr. Wickham."

"My family has, yes," replied Elizabeth. "Since your brother knows Mr. Wickham, I suppose I should have realized you would be familiar with him."

A pained expression came over Georgiana's countenance. "As familiar with the *gentleman* as I ever wish to be, yes." Georgiana paused, and some remembrance of pain came over her countenance before she shook it off in what Elizabeth could only call an angry fashion. "There is something of which I wish to speak to you of Mr. Wickham, for his offenses are a long and sad tale. But will you not share your family's story with me first? I understand from William that he has a central role in your family's woes."

While Elizabeth had no desire to relive her family's disgrace for a second time that week, she knew she could not refuse. And so, she began speaking, attempting to push all emotion away and relate her tale as dispassionately as she could, unlike the emotion-fraught relating she had given to Mr. Darcy. In contrast to her brother, Georgiana listened in silence, her only responses a gasp at certain parts of the story, or to pat Elizabeth's hand in a soothing fashion.

"Oh, Lizzy!" exclaimed Georgiana when Elizabeth fell silent. "How your family has suffered! I knew Mr. Wickham was depraved, but I never thought him bad enough to murder a man! And your poor sister!"

"I *do* miss my father," said Elizabeth with a sigh. "Very much. As for my sister . . ."

Elizabeth shrugged and smiled, though she was well aware it was a tepid effort at best. "Lydia and I were never close, you understand. Jane, my eldest sister, and I were always each other's dearest friends, while Kitty and Lydia were close."

"But you still *must* regret the loss of a sister!" exclaimed Georgiana.

"Of course I do," replied Elizabeth. "But it is very hard, as I also know that Lydia played a large role in our family's disaster, notwithstanding the fact that she is a silly, selfish girl."

At Georgiana's questioning glance, Elizabeth sighed and looked away. "Lydia was always a wild child, and Kitty followed her wherever she led. She had little understanding of propriety, and even less wish to know, for anything Jane or I said with dismissed. Mama, not being born a gentlewoman, had no notion of proper behavior either. Jane and I were routinely embarrassed by her excesses. She supported Lydia in everything, claiming it was just high spirits, never considering her youngest was on a path to ruin us all.

"I know her fall was Mr. Wickham's doing. But Lydia, in being allowed to continue in silliness and ignorance, contributed to it herself. While I can forgive her, I am also relieved the reminder of our disgrace is not among us any longer."

Georgiana was silent for a moment, attempting to understand Elizabeth's words. When she spoke, she was hesitant. "I suppose I can understand that, Lizzy, though I will own the thought of losing a sister is incomprehensible to one who never had one."

"That is understandable," said Elizabeth. She attempted a smile. "Having a sister—or even four—is not always enjoyable. There will always be vexations and sometimes outright arguments. Even between Jane and me, it was not always pleasant."

Georgiana nodded and changed the subject. "Did Mr. Wickham not attempt to ply his trade with you?" Flashing Elizabeth a smile, she added: "I cannot imagine he would find a beautiful woman like you not worth his time."

Though Elizabeth blushed at the praise, she attempted to push it to the side. "While I spoke with Mr. Wickham readily enough, he never attempted a closer relationship with me. I was there when we first made his acquaintance, for he came sometime after the arrival of the regiment to join their numbers. But while he was polite, he never tried to come to a closer friendship with me."

"Perhaps that is because he knew you would not be charmed as your sister was."

With a sigh, Elizabeth allowed Georgiana's supposition to be true. "Lydia was vulnerable to any man who spoke to her using pretty words, especially if they wore a red coat. She also spoke of being the first of her sisters to be married, even though she was the youngest. She truly was a thoughtless, stupid girl."

"I wish I could have made her acquaintance," said Georgiana. When Elizabeth turned a questioning glance at her, she explained: "I lack confidence at times. Some of Miss Lydia's confidence may have encouraged mine to appear."

"If you were able to separate the confidence from the silliness." Georgiana shot her a censorious look, but Elizabeth shook her head. "I love my sister yet, Georgiana. But by the time she was sundered from us, I will own I did not like her very much."

Georgiana subsided, thinking for some time before she essayed to speak again. When she did, her words shocked Elizabeth.

"Perhaps you are too harsh with your sister, Elizabeth. After all, you do not know what you might have done had Mr. Wickham focused his interest on you."

"I know I would not have allowed him such liberties with my person," averred Elizabeth. "Surely you would not have allowed such things yourself."

"There you would be incorrect."

For a moment, Elizabeth thought she had misheard her friend's statement. When Georgiana only continued to look at her with placid acceptance, Elizabeth could not help but look at her with astonishment.

"Mr. Wickham imposed himself upon you?" she finally managed to ask.

"Not in the manner of which you are thinking, Elizabeth," replied Georgiana. "While I do not know what I might have done had he pressed me to do so, I did not lose my innocence to him. But yes, I have *intimate* knowledge of exactly what kind of man Mr. Wickham is, and as such, I sympathize with your sister."

Elizabeth peered at Georgiana, wondering if the girl was simply attempting to make a point, speaking metaphorically rather than literally. But such hope could not be resolved, for to Elizabeth's eyes, she was entirely sincere.

"When did this happen?" asked Elizabeth after a moment.

"Two summers gone," was Georgiana's reply. "Will you allow me to tell you my tale?"

"Of course," replied Elizabeth.

Georgiana smiled, and nodded, and then fell into introspection. "Mr. Wickham was always known to me. Memories of Mr. Wickham are as old as my memories of William, and in the beginning, they were just as dear. Being many years older than myself, he was William's playmate. But Mr. Wickham was always attentive to me as well, for he played with me, often had a sweet to pass to me, made it a point to spend time with me when he was able to do so.

"In fact," continued Georgiana in a distant voice, "looking back on it now, I suspect he may have conceived the idea of pursuing me when he was yet naught but a boy."

A gasp escaped Elizabeth's lips. "So young?"

"I cannot know, of course. But the attentions I received from Mr. Wickham were different from the relationship I had with William. William was always happy to see me, for I was his precious little sister. William taught me to ride, helped me in my lessons, played with me whenever I entreated him. He truly was—is!—the perfect elder brother.

"By contrast, Mr. Wickham was always flattering, telling me how beautiful I was, kissing my hand when I became a young woman, plying me with presents and sweets. I wonder if he was always grooming me to have a good opinion of him, one he could exploit at a date and time of his choosing."

Georgiana paused and shrugged. "There is no way of knowing, of course, and I suppose it is not truly relevant to my story. Suffice to say that by the time my father passed away, I saw Mr. Wickham one final time at Pemberley, when he came to visit my brother. I now know it was to receive his payment in lieu of the Kympton living, though at the time I had no knowledge of such dealings. I knew nothing of him until last year.

"It was during the summer he intruded on my life. I had completed school and returned to Pemberley, where we entertained Mr. Bingley and his family for a short time. After they departed, my companion and I left Pemberley for a holiday at Ramsgate in eastern Kent. Mrs. Younge, my companion, was a serious woman, perhaps five and thirty years of age—a widow, or so she claimed. She was not an open woman, nor was she particularly friendly. But I trusted her, and I spent many a happy hour in her company.

"Then Mr. Wickham came."

Startled at the inference in Georgiana's words, Elizabeth said: "Do you suggest she was his confederate?"

"She was," said Georgiana. "We discovered later that they had been in each other's confidence. While it seems Mrs. Younge was, indeed, a widow, she had never been a gentlewoman as she asserted. Furthermore, she had been Mr. Wickham's paramour, and had applied to the position at his insistence, with the full intent of stealing my dowry."

Elizabeth could only shake her head. "Mr. Wickham's schemes are far more extensive than I ever expected. I merely thought he was a rake and a seducer, though his many debts in Meryton came to light after his death." A grimace curved Elizabeth's lips. "There was much hardship in the village when it became clear he would never pay what he owed."

"Yes, that is typical of Mr. Wickham. I know of several instances in which William paid Mr. Wickham's debts and settled his accounts.

"In this particular instance, I am sure you can understand what happened. He came to Ramsgate and proceeded to make himself agreeable to me. Such was his success that I agreed to an elopement."

Elizabeth gasped—this misstep was enough to ruin Georgiana in society for even contemplating such an action. Mr. Wickham was nothing more than the son of a steward!

"But you did not," said Elizabeth. "How did you extricate yourself?"

"It was through no virtue of mine, Lizzy. William joined us a day or two before our departure. I was so happy to see him, so happy to inform him of my understanding with a man I thought was his dearest friend. His reaction shocked me."

"Was he very angry?" asked Elizabeth.

"Furious," replied Georgiana. "But not at me. Mr. Wickham and Mrs. Younge received the brunt of his anger. The former left immediately and did not return, while the latter was dismissed and warned of being brought up on charges if she dared speak of the matter. Then we returned to London."

Georgiana paused and smiled, though it was tinged with pain. "I would not have you think that William was in any way unkind. In fact, he apologized to me many more times than I ever did to him. He claimed it was his fault that I had not known of Mr. Wickham's character, that I never would have been susceptible to his flattery, had I known of his character. In a certain sense, I suppose he is correct.

"But I knew. I had been taught by my father and my brother, and I knew it was wrong to accept Mr. Wickham's overtures. The blame cannot rest all on William's shoulders—I must bear some portion of it."

"Mr. Wickham bears the largest part," said Elizabeth. Her voice was almost a whisper, the tears rolling down her cheeks matching Georgiana's own.

"He does," replied Georgiana. "But I will not refuse to accept the blame for my own actions." Georgiana favored Elizabeth with a watery smile. "After all, I shall not learn how to behave properly if I do not accept the lessons I learn, shall I?"

"Very true," replied Elizabeth.

The two girls embraced, their tears mingling together, a common bond now tying them together. And for a time, Elizabeth was able to forget her worries, her certainty she had seen the last of Mr. Darcy. Though his sister's error had not been as egregious as *hers*, he could hardly hold Lydia's disgrace against her. Perhaps there was hope after all.

In all, the length of Georgiana's stay that day encompassed some hours. She did stay to take luncheon at the Gardiner house, and the early part of the afternoon was spent with the Gardiner children. They walked in the park, and all had a marvelous time of it. After they returned to the house, she said her goodbyes to Elizabeth and departed, leaving a more contented Elizabeth behind.

For a time Elizabeth was of a better frame of mind, and she could see that her aunt was happy with the development. She truly was not made for melancholy, and she was happy to prove it during the rest of that day, laughing and talking with her relations, reveling in the bosom of her family who had accepted her without reservation. For the first time in what seemed like days, Elizabeth was truly happy.

The next day was Friday, and the delivery of the mail saw a disruption of Elizabeth's state of mind. While she enjoyed receiving letters from Mary and Kitty, her mother's missives were often a trial. Mrs. Bennet had not taken her reduction in consequence and the loss of her home with any sanguinity, and she was not shy about informing them all of her opinions on the matter. The initial months after Elizabeth's departure for London had been characterized by her mother's continual harangues, berating Elizabeth for the loss of Longbourn due to her refusal of Mr. Collins's suit. The passage of time had moderated her mother's tone, though that was not always a cause for celebration either.

On this occasion, Elizabeth perused her mother's letter, noting the lack of spirits, the complaints of her nerves and the small house in which she was now forced to call home. There was a reference to Mr. Collins, as Elizabeth had expected, given the tone of the letter, but rather than the bitter recriminations, the railing against Charlotte Lucas for stealing their inheritance, Mrs. Bennet's words conveyed a sad regret, the kind which showed a truly defeated woman.

"What does your mother write?" asked Mrs. Gardiner when Elizabeth finally sighed and set the letter aside.

"What would you expect her to write?" asked Elizabeth with a wry smile which she knew did not deceive her aunt. "She regrets the loss of Longbourn, Lydia's disappearance, Jane's residence in the north with no contact, and her lack of consequence in her new home. I only hope she has managed to refrain from speaking of her laments to the ladies where they now live, or the neighborhood will quickly become inhospitable."

"Mr. Gardiner made very clear to her the consequences of doing so," said Mrs. Gardiner. "You need not worry for that."

Sighing, Elizabeth nodded and stared out the window, moodily thinking of the woman who had birthed her. "Though it is unlikely, I wish Mama could understand, even for an instant, that the loss of her husband and her home was in no small part due to her own actions in indulging my youngest sister."

"On some level, I believe your mother *does* understand." Elizabeth turned to Mrs. Gardiner, wondering as to her meaning. Mrs. Gardiner chuckled and shook her head. "She has not given me to understand this, Lizzy, and I dare say she will never be induced to own to her folly. But her melancholy in the letters I have received is such that I am certain she has not escaped self-reflection altogether."

Elizabeth considered her aunt's words. "Perhaps you are correct. This letter is as shattering as any letter I have ever had from her, even in the immediate aftermath of my departure."

Shaking herself free of her thoughts, Elizabeth turned back to her aunt. "I would not have you think I have no charity for my mother. I do. In fact, I have convinced myself that I must attempt to see matters from her perspective. She is my mother, and I remember the woman who played with me as a child, who called me her beautiful little girl, though her attention was much more firmly fixed on Jane was we grew older and she required Jane to rescue her. I hope Mama can put her feelings of depression aside and find happiness in that house." Elizabeth directed a wry smile at her aunt. "At least her constant fear of being resident in hedgerows has not come to pass. The cottage in which Mr. Bingley and Uncle installed her is not large, but it is quite comfortable."

"It is," agreed Mrs. Gardiner. Then she turned an appraising look on Elizabeth. "Then you would not object to inviting your mother to London for a time?"

"Of course not!" exclaimed Elizabeth. "I long to see my mother and sisters again."

"Then I will speak to Mr. Gardiner." Mrs. Gardiner smiled. "Perhaps it would be desirable to have them here for the Christmas season, but I do not think we can manage it. Your uncle is very busy at present and wishes to ensure the carriage is fit for a long journey. Perhaps they may join us in the New Year for the season. We do not move in exalted company, but perhaps we may find someone who will suit you girls."

Mrs. Gardiner shot a teasing gaze at Elizabeth. "Then again, I doubt we need to search for anyone in your case. You seem to have made quite a conquest, my dear."

Elizabeth could not help the heat which spread over her cheeks and down her neck. Though the thought of protesting her aunt's teasing occurred to her, the amusement with which Mrs. Gardiner regarded her informed her it would only serve to increase the teasing. As it was, the best course would be to direct the conversation back to her mother's proposed visit.

"Mama would appreciate a visit to London. It is my understanding from the letters I have received from Kitty and Mary that she has not managed to find many ladies as friendly as those in Meryton."

A sigh was Mrs. Gardiner's response. "That, unfortunately, is the truth, though I do not doubt that part of it is your mother's perception. Newcomers, especially a widow with two daughters, would be looked on with . . . Well, perhaps not exactly suspicion. But acceptance must take some time. One cannot expect your mother to be as friendly with the new ladies as she was with Lady Lucas or Mrs. Goulding, as they are acquaintances of longstanding."

"That is true," acknowledged Elizabeth. "In truth, I think it is best that they eschew society at present. My mother is, after all, still in half mourning. I am happy that Kitty seems to be content with her charcoals, and uncle was able to find a pianoforte to keep Mary occupied."

"I have heard that Mary has even begun to teach her a little."

"Perhaps she has," replied Elizabeth with a laugh. "But Kitty is not exactly an apt student. I have no doubt she would prefer to concentrate on her art."

"It is good that Kitty has discovered such an interest. Her years of chasing after Lydia undoubtedly left her with little identity of her own."

Elizabeth acknowledged that it was so and allowed the conversation to end. In the previous bleak months, Elizabeth had attempted to push thoughts of her mother and sisters to the back her mind to avoid thinking about that which brought her pain. Of late, however, her perspective was changing, and while it was still some months in the future, the possibility of seeing them again was agreeable. In fact, Elizabeth could allow that she was becoming excited at the thought.

The issue of what Mr. Darcy would think of her mother crossed Elizabeth's mind, but she once again firmly pushed the thought away. Not only had she not seen Mr. Darcy since she had made her confession to him, but she did not know whether he would wish to be known to Mrs. Bennet, even if he did return. There was no sense in thinking of matters which would only bring her pain.

CHAPTER VIII

*I*t was with a renewed sense of purpose that Elizabeth woke and went about her life the next day. Mr. Darcy may not decide she was suitable to become his wife, and should that be the case, Elizabeth decided there was nothing she could do. She, therefore, endeavored to put it from her mind. At least there were matters which kept her occupied in the intervening days.

"I understand you had planned to go to the hospital today," said her aunt, early that morning. "I wondered, however, if you would consider forgoing that today. Benjamin has a cold, and I could use your help here. Nurse also has a cold, which makes the situation more difficult."

Taken aback, Elizabeth's first instinct was to protest. But then her better nature asserted itself, and she reconsidered. Her aunt and uncle had done so much for her. There was nothing Elizabeth wished for more than to go to the hospital with the expectation of seeing Mr. Darcy again. But she could not refuse her aunt's request.

"Of course, I shall stay and assist you, Aunt," replied Elizabeth.

"You are a good girl, Lizzy," replied Mrs. Gardiner, leaning forward to embrace her. "I could not be happier that you are here with us."

Smiling, Elizabeth allowed herself to be led away. That Saturday was spent with the other children, whom her aunt had segregated away from her youngest in the hope they would not catch the same cold. Little Benjamin was upset at being separated from his siblings, but as he was also running a low fever, it was enough for his mother to keep him confined to his bed while she read to him and kept him occupied.

The other children were initially upset at their brother's illness until Elizabeth soothed them and assured them of his recovery. After that, Elizabeth played with the three children, inventing games for their amusement, reading their favorite stories, and even playing pianoforte with them. The girls quite enjoyed this last activity, though James, the Gardiners' eldest son, thought it an unfortunate activity for a boy.

"Oh, James," chided Elizabeth, shaking her head at the recalcitrant lad. "Many of the greatest masters in history were men. Do you not think they learned to play as children?"

The young boy looked at her, suspicion written on his countenance. "Masters? Which ones?"

"Herr Mozart, for example?" said Elizabeth. "Mozart wrote the music we were playing just now. Do you not think it was lively and beautiful?"

James nodded, though distracted as he looked at the music sitting on the instrument. "Should I learn to play, might I make music like this? "

Laughing, Elizabeth drew him to her. "Perhaps you might, though you would need to study very hard. Most of us, I believe, are content to simply learn to play the music. I believe it is only those who love music the most who feel the calling to write new music."

For the rest of their time that afternoon, James was more introspective than usual, which, interpreted, meant that he was introspective at all. Most boys of five years with whom Elizabeth had been acquainted were not known for their introspective nature. James, in particular, was much more likely to run than sit and read a book. Unfortunately, as the wind was strong that day and carried a hint of moisture, a trip to the park to spend his energy was not practicable.

It is not to be supposed that keeping three young children occupied for an entire day was an easy chore. This was especially true when the delights of the outside world were denied to them because of inclement weather. That day, seeing to the Gardiner children's amusement as she did, Elizabeth obtained a greater measure of respect for their nurse, who always found ways to keep them occupied.

As the afternoon waned and all of her ideas were used for their amusement, Elizabeth found herself in the Gardiner sitting-room room with the children, gathered around Mrs. Gardiner's nativity scene. It was a little set her husband had imported from Rome a few years previously as a gift for his wife. Although it was still early in December, her aunt had confided that she felt displaying the scene earlier helped to teach the children the true meaning of the holiday, rather than simply a time to receive gifts. It was to this topic that the conversation turned, and Elizabeth, knowing they were good children, willingly lent her own perspective to help them understand, particularly when the subject devolved into an argument.

"Why does Mama like this old thing so much?" demanded James, poking at the figure of one of the wise men. "It is not interesting. She will not allow me to play with them."

"It is because it is a nativity," said Abigail, the next eldest child with a disgusted shake of her head. Of the four children, it was usually James and Abigail who would argue. "It is important."

"Why is it important? They do not *do* anything. They are not as interesting as my soldiers."

The voice of the boy of five, of course, contained the surety that nothing was so important as toy soldiers. His sister, however, only glared at him for his stupidity, and Elizabeth, knowing she would say something which would provoke an argument, interrupted before she could respond.

"It is a depiction of the birth of our Lord, James."

"The story the pastor speaks of in church?" asked James, a hint of interest appearing in his tone.

"Yes," replied Elizabeth. She was impressed that he remembered, for he would only have been a boy of four the previous year. "You see," continued Elizabeth, pointing her finger at the manger, with the babe lying atop, "that is Jesus our Lord lying there. He was born in a manger about this time of year, in a stable in a land far away."

There was no mistaking James's interested gaze now. "What are these others?"

Patiently, Elizabeth endeavored to explain each one of the delicate porcelain figures, pointing to each one as she named them. As she explained, the children listened, enthralled — even the girls, who were older and already knew what each represented. As they spoke, Elizabeth felt a warmth enter her heart, the domestic scene one she would not have imagined not long before. A part of her heart suddenly longed to have this scene repeated, only with children of her own, with a man she loved. The image of Mr. Darcy settled in Elizabeth's consciousness, so real she could see him, hear him speak her name, and smell the scent of his cologne.

"Lizzy! Lizzy!"

Startled by the sound of her voice, Elizabeth blinked, looking down on the insistent face of James as he tugged on the sleeve of her gown. By his side, his sisters were no less curious about her lapse, though not as insistent in gaining her attention. Realizing she had been lost in her thoughts, Elizabeth looked away in embarrassment.

"Of what were you thinking, Lizzy?" asked Sophie, her eldest cousin.

"Nothing in particular," dissemble Elizabeth. "Just a stray thought."

"I have never seen someone smiling as they considered a random thought," said Abigail with an entirely unwarranted measure of slyness, in Elizabeth's opinion.

"Never you mind," replied Elizabeth, speaking before Abigail, who obviously suspected something, could further tease her.

"Who were the wise men?" asked James, pointing to one of the kings, lightly touching the crown adorning his head.

"We do not know," replied Elizabeth, "for the Bible does not say. It does say they traveled from far in the east bearing gifts for the Christ child."

"Gifts?" asked James. "Like my toy soldiers?"

Elizabeth smiled, for everything to James connected back to his army of soldiers. "No, James. The wise men, knowing that the Christ child was a very special child, brought gifts to reflect that respect and devotion for the child they knew would be the savior of the world. They brought gifts of gold, frankincense, and myrrh."

"Fran—Franken—Franksense?"

Laughing, Elizabeth patted her nephew's cheek with affection. "Frankincense."

She repeated it several times with him, helping him learn how to say the difficult word. In the end, he was grinning and repeating it back to her, clearly pleased he had mastered it. Then he turned serious again.

"What is Frankincense, Lizzy?"

"It is a kind of perfume, as is myrrh. In that time it was very costly, and was considered a kingly gift."

James's eyes widened. "That is why they were kings. Because only kings were rich enough to afford such gifts."

"Perhaps that is true," said Elizabeth, laughing once again.

"May we hear the nativity story?" asked Sophie.

"From the Bible?"

When the children all spoke excitedly in favor of the scheme, Elizabeth agreed and fetched the Gardiner family Bible. Then, opening it to the proper location, she began to read. Having heard it so many times, Elizabeth was almost able to recite it from memory. She reverently read every word from the thick tome, instilling into the words her love of the story and confidence in the tenets it taught. This was the true meaning of Christmas—the story of the savior, told to children, teaching them of the basic tenets of their faith. Elizabeth hoped that one day she would be surrounded by her own children, sharing this selfsame story. As she hugged Abigail to her side, she hoped it very much, indeed.

While Elizabeth spent those days in general contentment, it would not be long before she once again found herself attempting to grasp onto those feelings, as though they were smoke dissipating in the air. The next day was Sunday, and while Elizabeth hoped Mr. Darcy would visit that day, he did not come. Benjamin was much improved, which brought relief to his anxious mother, and as there were still activities with the children, Elizabeth did not think much of the still absent Mr. Darcy.

As her aunt could spare her again the next day, Elizabeth prepared to make her way to the hospital. Surely that day Mr. Darcy would once again be in attendance! The thought buoyed her, filling her with the feelings she had often experienced in his presence. Her anticipation thus heightened and her mood improved, Elizabeth prepared, unable to resist humming a happy Christmas carol under her breath.

"You appear to be quite happy today, Lizzy," observed her aunt as she watched Elizabeth putting on her gloves for her departure. "One might almost suspect you of anticipation. But I know it cannot be so, for you are simply to go to the hospital."

"And you do not think I can anticipate such an activity?" asked Elizabeth with a smile.

"Of course you are capable," replied Mrs. Gardiner. "However, while your time at the hospital is beneficial and fulfilling, I should not exactly call it exciting."

With a shrug, Elizabeth saw to her final preparations under her aunt's watchful eye. This did not deter Mrs. Gardiner, for she had more to say.

"Indeed, I might think your anticipation was due to the prospect of meeting with someone of your acquaintance. Now, who could that possibly be?"

"Goodbye, Aunt," said Elizabeth, bussing Mrs. Gardiner's cheek and refusing to rise to her bait.

"Have a wonderful day, Lizzy. I shall be waiting to hear all about it when you return home."

But the day at the hospital was not all Elizabeth had hoped it would be. Her journey there passed without incident, and she was assigned to certain tasks to which she applied herself with a will. Of the gentleman, there was no sign, and as there did not seem to be a meeting of the governors that day, she suspected he was not sequestered in an office, speaking of budgets, the children, or whatever other matters with which they must concern themselves. Elizabeth considered asking the matron if she knew anything of Mr. Darcy's presence, but she could not bring herself to make such an impertinent question. Thus, she attempted to put the matter of Mr. Darcy from her mind and concentrate on her tasks.

Though Elizabeth was friendly with most of the staff and volunteers who gave of their time to the institution, there were a few with whom she was most definitely not friendly. Most of the governors had little time for the young ladies who assisted, and Elizabeth typically had little contact with them. But there were some who were even less pleasant—some were downright mean-spirited.

The chief among these were two young ladies of about Elizabeth's age, or a little older. Lady Frances Graves was the daughter of an earl and every inch the nobleman's daughter, while her cousin, Miss Leticia Howard, spun in her orbit, her nose as high in the air as her cousin's. In truth, Elizabeth had little notion as to why they ever came to the hospital. They seemed to think any kind of labor beneath them as they rarely did anything other than speak together in haughty tones. Indeed, they were the masters of catty remarks to the other ladies about them, and they often seemed more of a hindrance than a help. Elizabeth wondered if their fathers forced them to come on occasion, though she did not see them often. If they did, the women could do with a little humility, for their behavior was trying and their pride quite beyond regulation.

"Can you believe the audacity of that dowdy little Miss Bennet?"

On an errand as she was for the matron, Elizabeth heard the voice of Lady Frances and stepped to the side of the hall, not knowing where the woman was. She did not wish to be seen, for she knew the ladies would turn their vitriol on her should they become aware of her presence.

"I consider little to be beyond her audacity," the voice of Miss Howard floated to Elizabeth's ears. "She seems quite eager to make a spectacle of herself."

The voice allowed Elizabeth to determine the location of the two women, inside a room a little further down the hall. Taking care not to be heard, Elizabeth edged forward, intending on bypassing the door and continuing on her way. She cared nothing for what either said of her, after all, so there was little to be gained by staying and listening.

"To think that she considers herself a match for Mr. Darcy, of all people! I can scarce believe it!"

Elizabeth froze. Had she been so open that the likes of these two cats were aware of her interest—or of Mr. Darcy's apparent interest in her?

"Not that she will succeed."

"Of course not!" An unladylike snort of disgust reached Elizabeth's ears. "Mr. Darcy has far too much dignity to fall for the machinations of the likes of her. Mr. Darcy's father was known to my father, you know, and Papa is an ally of Mr. Darcy's uncle, Lord Matlock. It is unthinkable that Mr. Darcy could consider such a woman for his wife."

"It is possible she might try to . . . arrange a situation which would engage his honor," warned Miss Howard.

Another snort was Lady Frances's reply. "I would be concerned for the gentleman if I did not already know that he has fended off fortune hunters since he entered society. If she should attempt something, I have no doubt she will discover him far superior to any stratagem she can muster."

"He *is* a handsome man," said Miss Howard. "Perhaps I should try my hand with him. He would be an eminently suitable husband, after all."

A silence ensued, awful to Elizabeth's feelings, and she thought of fleeing, certain she was about to be caught. When she heard the voices again, it was clear that Lady Frances was not precisely pleased with her cousin's suggestion.

"Perhaps it would be best should *I* set my sights on Mr. Darcy. He is not titled, it is true, but it is possible with Papa's assistance he might be the recipient of one."

"The Darcys have refused titles in the past," cautioned Miss Howard. From her tone, Elizabeth caught a hint of subservience and suspected that Lady Frances had fixed her with a scowl during her silence.

"It is nothing that cannot be overcome," said Lady Frances, and Elizabeth had the impression of her waving her hand as if swatting away an annoying gnat. "I am certain a wife can convince him to accept. It would increase his importance in society. What gentleman does not wish for that?"

The ladies giggled together, though Elizabeth thought it was forced in the case of at least one of them. Perhaps it was best to leave after all.

"Yes, I think he will do," said Lady Frances after a moment, as Elizabeth began her retreat. "And should Miss Bennet think to attempt to interfere, well I am certain I can deal with her. A pointed comparison between the two of us is certain to remind Mr. Darcy of who is superior. I dare say she will flee back to Cheapside with her tail between her legs if I put my mind to her humiliation."

Elizabeth fled, certain she did not wish to hear any of their insults. Careful to make no noise, she walked past the room in which they were speaking, noting the door was pulled to, though not closed, and continued on her way.

It had long been acknowledged that Miss Elizabeth Bennet was not the sort of woman to allow another to frighten her. One of her favorite phrases had always been to claim that any attempt to intimidate her was met with an increase of her courage sufficient to withstand any attack. Under normal situations, she would have shrugged off whatever was said about her, content to relegate it to jealousy, spite, or simple unkindness.

But this situation was different. Their unkind insinuations and vile taunts hit to the heart of Elizabeth's present insecurity. She knew she was not any less estimable a woman than the two who spoke their insults and looked down on all. But her situation, the loss of her father, of her home, had left her feeling bereft, knowing she was still the daughter of a gentleman, but fearing she would never again be acknowledged as such. Surely such considerations—her father's lack of prominence when he had been alive, her lack of dowry and connections, her relative anonymity—must be of material importance to a young man of Mr. Darcy's stature.

Could she expect him, the scion of an old and wealthy line with ties to the nobility, to settle for a girl such as she, one without fortune or even a name? Elizabeth attempted to tell herself that Mr. Darcy was not of such ilk. But her situation and his continued absence eroded her confidence, such that by the time her departure drew nigh, all the progress she had made since Georgiana's visit had dissipated like mist on a sunny day.

As the carriage rolled through the streets back toward Gracechurch Street, Elizabeth felt the last of her confidence slipping away as if it had never existed. There was no point in hoping—she may as well wish to hold the moon in the palm of her hand. It was impossible that Mr. Darcy would ever offer her his heart, let alone his hand, and it was nothing less than foolishness to wish for it.

Tears spilled from Elizabeth's eyes, and she dashed them away angrily. It would have been better had she never even met the man. Then she would have no notion of what she was missing, of what she could never have.

The pealing of a bell pierced Elizabeth's consciousness, forcing her self-pity to the back of her mind for the moment, and she looked out the window, seeing the church just up the street from her uncle and aunt's house. And suddenly a longing filled her, and she banged on the roof of the carriage, signaling the driver to stop.

Opening the door herself, Elizabeth stepped down to the bewilderment of the unfortunate driver. Without a word, she stepped toward the sanctuary of the Lord's house, yearning for the solitude it would offer her.

"Miss Bennet!" the voice of the worried driver reached her ears. "Your aunt and uncle are waiting for you at the house!"

"I shall not be long," called Elizabeth. "You may return to my uncle's house."

Then she was inside the church, taking no notice of the chagrinned Jacobs or the impropriety of what she had just told him. She had no thought but to reach the front pews, to sink down on the kneeling bench and pour out her frustrations and sorrows to the Almighty. Had there been anyone in evidence, it was very possible her display might have set tongues to wagging. But it was blessedly deserted—even the parson was not in evidence.

When she reached her destination, Elizabeth settled gingerly on the pew first. She had no notion of what she wished to do. Prayer was an attractive notion, to plead for her salvation from the heartache she suspected would break her forever. But how did one pray for such a thing? Elizabeth had attended church all her life, had recited the prayers, sung the hymns, given of herself to the service of God. But this was more personal than a Sunday worship service. She was a lone woman, beseeching the Almighty for her salvation. Would He even hear?

Whether she would be heard was something she could not

determine. But the compulsion to obtain comfort was overpowering. Feeling a little self-conscious, Elizabeth fell to her knees on the bench and bowed her head over, clasping her hands together tightly. Her thoughts were a jumble, and though she reached out to God for succor, she could not be certain exactly what she requested. Peace, perhaps? Or happiness, Mr. Darcy's return, or simply to have her sorrow taken from her. She did not know.

How long Elizabeth stayed in that attitude, she could never say. It may have been mere moments, or it may have been hours. However long it was, Elizabeth gradually became aware of footsteps approaching her, the soles clacking against the tiles and echoing between the benches and walls on either side of her. Ignoring it, Elizabeth continued to pour out her very soul, asking for assistance in her time of need.

And then she heard a soft voice: "Miss Bennet?"

Slowly, Elizabeth raised her head from her clasped hands and looked up, wondering if this was an answer to her prayers. It was Mr. Darcy. And he was looking at her with an expression of worry, mixed with love and longing. He had finally come.

CHAPTER IX

*I*t was the merest chance that Darcy happened to notice the Gardiner carriage as his own drove down the avenue. Even then he might not have stopped had he not seen the driver standing beside the equipage, wringing his hands. While it might be nothing more than the cold, the look of worry on the man's face belied Darcy's supposition and caused him to call out to his own driver to stop on the side of the road.

Alighting from the carriage, Darcy approached the unfortunate man, who, seeing Darcy, bowed, knuckling his forehead. "Mr. Darcy, sir."

"Is there some trouble?"

A glance at the church informed Darcy that whatever problem existed had to do with the church before them. He did not relent in his questioning gaze, which ultimately persuaded the man to submit.

"It is Miss Bennet, sir. She asked the carriage to stop and hurried into the church without a by your leave. Her aunt and uncle are waiting for her and will become worried before long."

"I shall bring her home," said Darcy. He smiled. "I was on my way to your master's house anyway. You may go on home."

Jacobs looked at him, doubt coloring his features. In the end, he must have decided that Darcy was trustworthy, for he touched his hat. "Thank you, sir. I will tell the master and his wife what has become of their niece."

Then, with a single reproachful look at the church doors, he scrambled atop the box and flicked the reins, sending the carriage into motion. Darcy, however, ignored him in favor of the church, and with a firm resolve, stepped inside.

The light in the building was dim, only a few of the sconces being lit, casting a warm, though faint, glow on the inside of the church. It was not so large or so ornate as the building near his own home, unsurprising, given the part of town in which it stood. Those primped peacocks of Mayfair demanded the best for their place of worship, and it was designed accordingly. Such conceit was the same no matter where one went.

As his eyes adjusted to the light, Darcy's gaze caught sight of a small figure in the second pew, head bowed in the attitude of prayer. His heart beginning to beat in anticipation of seeing the exquisite Miss Bennet once again, he walked down the aisle, taking care to remain as silent as he could.

When he had reached her side, Darcy looked tenderly down at the woman who had captured his imagination and invaded his very soul. She was, indeed, in an attitude of prayer, her lips moving in silent words. A moment of observation brought a frown to Darcy's face, for she seemed to be in the throes of some great disturbance of mind, one which only an appeal to the Savior himself could resolve.

"Miss Bennet?"

Darcy's questioning address was barely audible, and for a moment Darcy thought she had not heard him. But slowly her head rose from the bench in front of her, and she gazed at him in incomprehension. For a moment, neither spoke, Darcy drinking in the sight of her, wondering that he had not realized before now how much he had missed her in the past few days when he had been unable to attend her.

"Mr. Darcy? How came you to be here?"

"I might ask you the same thing, Miss Bennet," said Darcy with a smile. "I happened to notice your uncle's carriage driver and stopped to speak to him. You have given him quite a fright."

A flush spread over her cheeks which Darcy found quite fetching. He gestured to the bench, and she nodded, scuttling back from her position on the kneeling bench to sit erect, as if ready to flee. Darcy took his own seat beside her, turning half toward her. He noted, in a corner of his mind which was not consumed by her presence, a hint of the scent she wore today, some blend he could not quite determine, but which he found lovely. Her hair was slightly mussed from her previous attitude, but that did not detract from her perfection in his eyes. She was lovely in every way.

"I appears there is something dreadfully amiss, enough to cause you to seek solace in the house of the Lord."

He color rose again, but she managed to shake her head. "There is something which has been plaguing my mind, but it is of no consequence now." She cast him a sidelong look. "It is a little late for a call, is it not?"

Delighted at her ability to descend to teasing on a whim, Darcy replied: "When I met with your uncle this afternoon, he invited me to dinner. I was on my way to keep that engagement when I followed you in here."

Playfulness suddenly turned to bafflement. "You are come to dine with us tonight?"

"I am," replied Darcy. "Is my presence offensive?"

"Oh, no, sir!" said she, her eyes widening in consternation. She then withdrew into herself, her eyes not quite meeting his. "With your absence these past days, I was not certain I would see you again. In fact, I quite expected I would not."

"You thought I would not come again?" asked Darcy, wondering how she had come to that conclusion.

"No," whispered she.

"I know not how you could have come to such an opinion," said Darcy. "I would never abandon you."

Miss Bennet looked up at him, surprise evident in her mien. "But I am in no way suitable to be your acquaintance. Does my account of my family's troubles not give you pause?"

"It might, should I lay blame for the actions of a sister on you. It would be unfair of me to do so, would it not?"

"You are very different from other gentlemen I have known, sir," said Miss Bennet, appearing bewildered. "Any other man would stay far away from me and keep his sister even farther."

"Any other man is not in love with you, Miss Bennet."

Then on the impulse of the moment, Darcy leaned forward and pressed his lips against hers. Miss Bennet's eyes flared open for the briefest moment, and then she sighed and allowed her hand to rest on his arm, which he had raised to cup her cheek. The kiss was entirely chaste, for Darcy knew she would become frightened if he attempted to deepen the intimacy of it. He broke it much sooner than he would have wished, leaning forward to rest his forehead against hers. She sighed and closed her eyes, a half smile formed on her lips.

"I should apologize for my imprudent action, Miss Bennet."

"You should," agreed she, still not opening her eyes.

"I find that I cannot."

Finally, the lids of her glorious eyes parted, and the beauty of her gaze rested on him. Whereas her look was usually sharp and inquisitive, she appeared languid at present, as if boneless and unable to move. But he knew that mind of hers was as sharp as ever.

"Why can you not apologize, sir?"

"Because I have yearned to do that for a long time now."

Her eyes sought the floor, her embarrassment acute. "You have?" Her voice was barely audible.

"Yes. Though I cannot state exactly when the desire made itself known, I am certain it was within days of making your acquaintance."

"Oh," was the only reply she could muster.

"Now, Miss Bennet—I should like to know why you thought you would never see me again. Have I given you any reason to believe in my inconstancy?"

"I have not seen you since the day of my confession, Mr. Darcy," said she, a challenge evident in her voice. "Was that not reason enough to suspect I had scared you away?"

Belatedly Darcy realized how it looked from her perspective, and he cursed himself for not considering her feelings. He had been so consumed by finished his business and setting into motion those things which would bring her pleasure that he did not stop to consider how she would feel he abandoned her. But he could not speak of such things, for he did not wish her to know of them at the present time.

"What of my words on our parting? Did they not promise I would return?"

"I knew not how to interpret them. A little time without seeing you brought them more into doubt."

"You have my apologies, Miss Bennet," said Darcy. "I did not think clearly and gave you a reason to doubt me. In fact, I have been engaged in business, ensuring that I will be at leisure. I assure you that I am not going anywhere."

"No?" asked Miss Bennet, the curve of her smile enchanting him beyond all resistance.

He leaned forward again and captured her lips in another kiss. Whereas the first was chaste, this one was much more aggressive, not harsh, but carrying the wealth of his feelings. And Miss Bennet, though it was clear she had no experience in such activities, she was a quick study, her lips moving against his, the tip of her tongue grazing against his lips.

It was the final sensation which provoked Darcy to end the kiss, pulling away panting, unaware he had become so short of breath. A part of his mind was filled with satisfaction that she was as affected as he was. But they were not married—not even courting—and even if they had been, a church was no setting for such activities.

"Does that convince you?" asked he.

"You may be a rake," replied she, an impish grin fixed on him.

"Minx!" exclaimed Darcy. "What must I do to convince you?"

"Another demonstration might do the trick."

Much as he wished to do so, Darcy decided he must act with some thought for decorum. "I think such activities in a church would likely be frowned upon."

Her countenance grew pale at the reminder of where they were, and her eyes shot around the church, looking to see if anyone had witnessed their interlude. Near the door to the vestry stood the parson, apparently having entered unknown to them both. The man was obviously known to Miss Bennet, for he smiled at her, while at the same time directing a pointed look in Darcy's direction. He did not speak, however, and for that Darcy was grateful.

If he had thought her blush prominent before, it was nothing compared to the deep redness which spread over her face at the knowledge they had been observed. She nodded back at the parson and then averted her eyes, seeming unable to meet anyone's gaze. Darcy took pity on her.

"I believe your uncle and aunt will be concerned for you. Perhaps we should return to your uncle's house?"

A brief nod was Miss Bennet's response. Taking the hand he extended to her, she rose and curtseyed to the parson, before allowing Darcy to put her hand in the crook of his arm. He led her from the church and out into the street beyond, Darcy signaling to his coachman to precede them up the street. As they walked, Darcy found his eyes drawn to her, and was gratified when she seemed to be in the same straits.

"I must own to some curiosity, Miss Bennet," said Darcy, prompting her to look up at him. "It is understandable that you would wonder over my return given the circumstances. Please excuse me if I misspeak, but I sense there is something more to it than you have related. Will you not share it with me?"

When she colored yet again, Darcy knew he had guessed correctly. But then she attempted to evade his question.

"As I informed you, I thought you had been chased away by my family's past."

Darcy watched Miss Bennet, watching for any hint she was dissembling. The way she blushed and looked away told him all he needed to know, and he wondered why she would not confide in him. Then she sighed and turned back to him, proceeding to relate in a hesitant voice what had happened that afternoon with Lady Frances and Miss Howard. Darcy could not help but snort with disgust at what he heard, though he was not surprised in the slightest. The ladies in question possessed a reputation in London for insupportable behavior. It was likely for that reason they remained unmarried after two seasons each. Many gentlemen did not care much for their wives, marrying for connections and fortune. But even the most disinterested man must not wish to marry a shrew.

"The words of those ladies concerned you?" prompted Darcy.

"I usually do not care for the opinions of others, Mr. Darcy," said Miss Bennet. "But I will own that their words struck a chord. Most men would wish for the things they can provide. I am naught but a poor woman, living in London on the sufferance of her aunt and uncle's generosity. If you wished for more, who am I to blame you?"

"Have I ever given you any reason to suppose that I wish for such things?"

Miss Bennet did not hesitate to shake her head. Darcy stopped their progress and turned to her, his finger touching her chin and tilting her head up so that she would meet his eyes.

"I am happy to hear it, Miss Bennet. In the future, I hope you will release your insecurity, for I have no interest in such ladies. Let their words trouble you no more. They are only due my civility. I intend to show you so much more."

A slight nod was her response, as more seemed to be quite beyond her capabilities at the present moment. With a nod of satisfaction, confident the fullness of his meaning had been understood, Mr. Darcy grasped her hand again, placed it on his arm, and continued down the boulevard. Within a few moments, they had arrived at the Gardiners' townhouse and the warmth of light and love which awaited them there.

"Lizzy!" exclaimed her Aunt Gardiner as they entered.

Mrs. Gardiner stepped forward to embrace Elizabeth, who was obliged to release Mr. Darcy's arm while her aunt fussed over her. Her immediate need for closeness quenched, Mrs. Gardiner drew back to arms' length, her eyes inspecting every inch of Elizabeth, who accepted the scrutiny, knowing she had worried her dear relation.

"Jacobs came with a story of your flight into the church—I was about to go looking for you."

"I am well, Aunt," said Elizabeth, smiling to show her the truth of her assertion. "Mr. Darcy collected me and escorted me home."

"It seems he did," said Mrs. Gardiner, turning her attention to the gentleman. "We are much obliged to you, Mr. Darcy. I do not know what happened with my niece, but she usually does not feel the need to seek the sanctity of our church on a whim."

"I was happy to be of service, Mrs. Gardiner," said Mr. Darcy with a bow.

Thanking him again, Mrs. Gardiner turned to Elizabeth, who for a moment thought her aunt might press the issue. She was thus relieved when Mrs. Gardiner did nothing more than inviting them into the parlor where they could warm themselves by the fire. It was with a sense of amusement that Elizabeth followed her aunt—though they were two entirely different women, at that moment Elizabeth thought she saw an echo of her mother's nerves in Mrs. Gardiner's reaction to her return.

Soon, after she had been bustled upstairs to change her gown to something more suitable to an evening in company, she was seated with Mr. Darcy in front of a crackling fire, a cup of mulled wine held in her hand. Mrs. Gardiner clucked around them for a few moments, speaking of how happy she was to have Mr. Darcy with them and Elizabeth returned to her. And after a few moments, she excused herself, citing the need to check with the cook regarding dinner.

"Mr. Gardiner had a matter of business which required his attention and is now in the study. I do not believe he will be long." She directed a stern glare at them, the effect of which was ruined by the trembling of her laughing lips and the brightness of her eyes. "Can I trust you both alone together while I complete some tasks?"

Embarrassment seemed to be her constant companion since Mr. Darcy found her in the church, which delayed Elizabeth's response. Mr. Darcy, however, seemed to have no such difficulty, for he grinned at Mrs. Gardiner and nodded in Elizabeth's direction.

"You may wish to hurry your return, Mrs. Gardiner, for I do not know how long I can resist your beguiling niece."

Though Elizabeth looked at the gentleman with wonder, Mrs. Gardiner laughed gaily. "I am happy to hear it, sir. If my sister had been present, she would have assured you were locked in this room together until you came to an agreement. As it is, I shall leave the door open, for I know Lizzy would die of mortification should I embarrass her."

As Mrs. Gardiner left the room, Mr. Darcy turned his eye on Elizabeth and fixed her with a smile of true amusement. "Perhaps I should arrange to meet this lady as soon as possible. If she is willing to leave me alone with her daughter, I must applaud her, for she only forwards my own designs."

"For shame, sir!" said Elizabeth, reclaiming a little of her impertinence. "I know not if I should continue to associate with such a reprobate as you."

Mr. Darcy laughed. "That puts me in mind of my cousin, Colonel Fitzwilliam, for I have often referred to him as a reprobate."

"Then I shall anticipate meeting him. Is he with your aunt and uncle at their estate?"

A shaken head was his response, accompanied by what Elizabeth interpreted as being a hint of concern. "Anthony is a colonel with the cavalry, Miss Bennet, and is currently on the continent fighting against the French."

"You must worry for him."

"Not as much as we used to." Mr. Darcy squeezed her hand, which he had taken when Mrs. Gardiner left the room and still not relinquished. "He is now assigned to Wellesley's staff, and is not leading men into battle."

A pause was followed by Mr. Darcy's grin, and he said: "I suspect such a posting does not suit Anthony's sense of the heroic—no doubt he will invent stories from whole cloth which are much more exciting than the reality of directing battle from afar. But it causes his mother to worry less for him, though that concern is not completely extinguished."

"Then I hope he is returned safely and swiftly." Elizabeth directed an arch look at her companion. "Thus far I have only been introduced to your sister. I hope to make the acquaintance of all your relations."

"And I shall anticipate introducing you," said Mr. Darcy. "My relations will love you, I am certain—especially my aunt."

"Why should your aunt take to me more than any others?" asked Elizabeth.

"Because your character is much like hers, Miss Bennet. My cousins have all inherited her teasing manner to some extent, though my uncle is much more like me."

Their solitude lasted for some time, and they used it to good advantage, speaking of several subjects. Mr. Darcy spoke of his family, specifically the earl's family and his mother's sister, Lady Catherine. Elizabeth was particularly interested to hear of the lady, given Mr. Collins's words concerning his patroness. Surely the man's sycophancy had led him to exaggerate her good qualities to an exceptional degree, and hearing of her from Mr. Darcy gave her a clearer — albeit similar — picture of her character.

"As I recall, you mentioned that your aunt was unhappy with you at present."

"That is true," replied Mr. Darcy with a rueful shake of his head. "Knowing the true extent of the matter may cause you to rethink your association with me, so I beg you not to ask me to speak of it."

Though he claimed a desire to avoid the subject, the laughter in his eyes told Elizabeth he had no objection to speaking of it. Intrigued, Elizabeth could not help but tease: "I beg you to inform me of the matter directly! It would be disastrous for me to learn of it only after it is too late!"

Laughter burst from both of their breasts, bringing Mrs. Gardiner to the door to look in on them, no doubt curious as to the reason for their mirth. Though she did not enter, Elizabeth could see the tender and hopeful smile with which she was favored before her aunt turned away.

"Then I shall do so," said Mr. Darcy, "though I warn you it is not for the faint of heart. You see, Miss Bennet, I refused to marry her daughter. You may now despise me at your leisure."

Struck with laughter though she was, Elizabeth was puzzled as to his meaning. "Indeed, I do not despise you. In fact, I am rather pleased you did not. But I am confused, for is it not the prerogative of the man to propose to the lady? Did she attempt, in some way, to force your hand?"

"In a manner of speaking," replied Mr. Darcy. "You see, she has long claimed that my engagement to my cousin was a matter decided between herself and her sister, who was my mother. Many were the times she extolled our cradle arrangement with the surety of one who brooks no opposition as if it were an established matter.

"But my mother never agreed to it, regardless of what Lady Catherine claims, and no contract was ever created to bind us together. Every spring I visit Rosings — Lady Catherine's estate — to deal with matters of the estate, the books, tenant issues, and the like. And every year she has hounded me about the engagement, demanding I finally propose to her daughter.

"It finally reached a head last year, for when I arrived, I immediately knew she was determined that it was to be the year I finally capitulated. To Lady Catherine's chagrin, I had no intention of being coerced."

Elizabeth erupted in gales of laughter. "Given what I have heard of the lady, I cannot imagine she accepted your refusal with any degree of serenity."

"That, my dear Miss Bennet, is a massive understatement. When she confronted me, I refused her entreaties and declined to listen to any subsequent demands. She would not desist, so I finally left the estate. I am certain her voice could be heard all the way to London, so incensed was she."

"Then she has disowned you," said Elizabeth with a smirk.

Mr. Darcy looked skyward. "Disown is a strong word, Miss Bennet, for there is nothing for her to disown me from. She assaulted my uncle, demanding he support her and force me to marry her daughter. Unfortunately for Lady Catherine, my uncle has long been accustomed to ordering her to silence—he is the only one who commands her respect. He chased her back to Rosings with a bee in her ear, informing her that I am my own man and could act as I pleased. The only contact I have had from her in months is a lecture via letter on a monthly basis, reminding me of my 'duty' and demanding my compliance. While I read the first few, the rest have been consigned to the fire unopened."

"It is no doubt a good place for them, Mr. Darcy."

With a wide grin, Mr. Darcy leaned forward. "So you see, Miss Bennet, I too have some relations which cause me to blush at times. I know hardly any families without at least one member who causes embarrassment. Mine is a shrewish old lady who gives advice without regard to being asked for it, and often without any experience in the subject about which she pontificates. So you do not have all the embarrassing relations to yourself!"

Before Elizabeth could reply, her uncle and aunt entered the room, both grinning at Elizabeth and Mr. Darcy. "There seemed to be plenty of mirth emanating from this room," commented Mr. Gardiner. "Do you care to share your jests with us?"

"We were speaking of embarrassing relations," replied Elizabeth.

"Lizzy!" scolded Mrs. Gardiner.

"Actually," said Mr. Darcy, looking at Elizabeth with amusement, "in this instance, the relation is one of *mine*. And I dare say Aunt Catherine is far more embarrassing than any ten of your relations!"

"I assure you, Mr. Darcy," said Mr. Gardiner in a dry tone, "you have never met my sister, so I urge you not to judge the matter until you have."

They all laughed at Mr. Gardiner's reply. Elizabeth, who knew possibly better than anyone here how difficult her mother could be, could only shake her head, for it was true. The love Elizabeth had for her mother had never been in question—sometimes she did not truly *like* the way her mother behaved, which was one of the reasons their relationship had been so difficult over the years.

"While I am sure you have a great knowledge of your relation," said Mr. Darcy, "we shall see, in the end, who is correct. Now, I have come here tonight, not only to partake of your excellent dinner, Mrs. Gardiner, but also with an invitation. Georgiana and I would be pleased if you would consent to join us at Darcy house for the Christmas celebration this year."

While she was excited at the prospect, Elizabeth looked to her aunt and uncle, who had each turned to the other. In the manner of couples long and happily married, a wealth of meaning seemed to pass between them in only a few glances, and Mr. Gardiner turned to Mr. Darcy to make their response.

"We would, of course, be pleased to accept, Mr. Darcy. But as you know, we have several small children we would not wish to impose upon you."

"Not at all, Mr. Gardiner," said Mr. Darcy. "It has been too long since children roamed the halls of Darcy house. And while I hope it is not too long before it happens again, Georgiana and I would be pleased to host *all* your family."

It was all Elizabeth could do not to gape at the man's blatant reference to a hope of future felicity with her. Luckily her surprise prevented her from the necessity of feeling as embarrassed. It could not be said, however, that she was able to escape her uncle and aunt's delighted grins.

"In that case, we would be happy to accept."

"Excellent!" cried Mr. Darcy. "Then it is settled. I am anticipating it very much!"

The way he looked at her informed Elizabeth of his sentiments, and she found that she returned them in every particular. They spent the rest of the evening in lively conversation. And Elizabeth forgot all about the devastation under which she had suffered only earlier that day. She was far too engaged in attending Mr. Darcy's every word to remember anything but her current bliss.

CHAPTER X

*I*t was nothing less than amazing, thought Elizabeth to herself over the next several days, how a small change in circumstances could bring about such a profound change in outlook. Not that the acknowledged love of a good man was a small matter, she supposed. But after so many days of regretting the loss of his good opinion, wishing for the ability to change history, the simple fact of his present assurances was enough to raise her from the deepest despair to the heights of happiness.

"I ought to have judged better," said Mr. Darcy ruefully. Elizabeth had been reluctant to speak of the matter. But Mr. Darcy, eager to assure her of his regard, had insisted she inform him in more detail the days after her confession. "I had no notion you would take my departure as evidence I was disgusted by what happened to you and your family."

"There is no need to consider the matter further, Mr. Darcy," said Elizabeth. "It is clear I did not trust you like I should have, so my suffering was my own doing."

"But it is entirely understandable you would think so. I should have informed you in no uncertain terms that I do not hold your sister's transgressions against her." Mr. Darcy smiled down at her, patting her hand as they continued to walk in the park near her uncle's house. "My only defense is that I thought I had been open enough in my admiration that my feelings were not in question."

"Your admiration *was* open, Mr. Darcy," replied Elizabeth quietly. "But few men could withstand such proof of family weakness."

"There is *one* who can," replied Mr. Darcy. When he looked down at her, his heart was in his eyes, and Elizabeth found herself rendered mesmerized by the sight. "I do not consider what happened to you a family weakness. It is clear it is your sister who transgressed. Why should her actions affect you and your other sisters?"

While Elizabeth agreed with him, her heart was too full to say anything further on the subject. She had little desire to speak of what Lydia had done, particularly since he had done her the singular honor of absolving her of all blame. Instead, Elizabeth changed the subject.

"What occupied you during the days you were absent, sir? Previous to that time I had seen you almost daily."

"Matters of business," said Mr. Darcy. "There were certain things I hoped to accomplish as soon as may be, and which required my full attention. The sooner completed, the sooner I would be in a position to focus my attention once again on you."

While Elizabeth listened to his explanation with interest, she noted how vague it was. She turned to look in his direction, noting how he was looking away, and she wondered if he was being evasive. For a moment she thought to press him on the matter. In the end, she decided to leave it alone, preferring to simply enjoy his company.

And happy Elizabeth was. Such times in Mr. Darcy's company were once again a daily occurrence after that. They often met at the hospital, for Mr. Darcy was once again regular in his attendance, and they resumed the practice of going thither together with Georgiana. They met at the Gardiners' house, Elizabeth and Mrs. Gardiner visited Georgiana at Darcy house, and there often walks, trips to various attractions, dinners and the like to occupy Elizabeth's time. How it had all come about, Elizabeth could not quite determine. Young women who came from disgraced families did not end as the beloved of a man of society such as Mr. Darcy. Yet, there it was.

"I hope that I am not putting the cart before the horse, Mr. Darcy," said Elizabeth on another occasion. She blushed, the words having come out in a rush and without forethought. But his eyes were now on her, and she could not take the words back now. "I merely wondered what your family would think of your current . . . interest in me."

The gentleman's reply removed any thought her question was

impertinent. "You do not put the cart before the horse in any way, Miss Bennet."

A few moments later, after he had seemingly gathered himself, Mr. Darcy continued to speak: "Georgiana is the most important member of my family, and as you know, she considers you a friend already. "Mr. Darcy paused and laughed. "In fact, I should be afraid for my safety if I did not make you her sister, for she has been quite demanding."

"She has?" asked Elizabeth, trying to reconcile his account with shy, dear Georgiana.

"It surprised me too!" exclaimed Mr. Darcy. "But there it is. As for the rest of my family, I believe my cousins would be nothing but happy for me, and while my uncle might be skeptical at first, he and my aunt would soon come to see your worth. The true problem would, of course, be Lady Catherine."

"Ah, yes," said Elizabeth, smiling at him mischievously. "Should I travel to Kent to ask her ladyship's permission to marry you?"

Mr. Darcy laughed and shook his head. "It would matter not at all how you asked, Miss Bennet, for permission would be denied, and her denial would not be spoken with anything other than insults and exclamations of her daughter's prior claim."

"It seems to me, Mr. Darcy," said Elizabeth, "that our marriage would actually be of benefit for your cousin. Perhaps she would be happier if her mother no longer pushed her toward you."

"You may be correct," said Mr. Darcy with a heavy sigh. "Or it would had I any confidence that Lady Catherine would not immediately start pushing Anne toward any man with a title in the hope of making a better match for her just to spite me."

"That is a strange notion," said Elizabeth. "How could she seriously think such a thing would affect you? Your cousin marrying another man would not affect *you*, after all."

"Perhaps not, and I agree with you. But it is so very much like my aunt that I suspect that is exactly the way she would act."

"Miss de Bourgh is of age?"

"That is so. But Anne does not have the strength to oppose her mother." Mr. Darcy paused, seemingly in thought. "I shall consider the matter. Perhaps my uncle might be persuaded to intervene."

The matter was dropped and not revisited, but for some time after their conversation, Mr. Darcy was quiet. Elizabeth knew she had awakened a persistent concern for his cousin in Mr. Darcy, and she hoped something could be done to assist the young woman. Though

Elizabeth had never met her, in some strange way, she felt a kinship with Miss de Bourgh. Perhaps it was Elizabeth's knowledge of Mr. Collins and her understanding of Lady Catherine's behavior from both Mr. Darcy and Mr. Collins. Either way, she hoped she would have the pleasure of making Miss de Bourgh's acquaintance sometime in the future.

One matter she had not foreseen was something her aunt said the day after her reunion with Mr. Darcy. As they sat at some needlework in the parlor that day, Elizabeth could feel her aunt's eyes on her, knew her aunt was considering what she wished to say.

"If I was not already certain Mr. Darcy did not propose," said she at length, "I might think you already engaged, considering your behavior."

When Elizabeth did not respond, Mrs. Gardiner gave her a severe look. "Well, Niece? *Has* Mr. Darcy proposed?"

"He has not, Aunt. But I am now convinced he will."

One elegant eyebrow rose, as Mrs. Gardiner continued to gaze at Elizabeth. "Has he promised to propose?"

"Not in so many words," confessed Elizabeth. "But we have spoken, though in an oblique sort of manner, of marriage and the future."

Mrs. Gardiner laughed and shook her head. "Only you, Lizzy." She turned a mock frown on Elizabeth. "Are you not aware that it is just not done to speak of such things before the proposal has been offered?"

"Perhaps not, Aunt," replied Elizabeth, unaffected by her aunt's teasing for the first time in what felt like weeks. "But after Mr. Darcy's return, I think we both wished to understand exactly where we stood. I do not complain of a slight breach in propriety."

"Nor should you be. I am quite happy for you Lizzy. You know how fond of you your uncle and I are — Mr. Darcy is a finer man than we ever hoped for you. You will be a very happy woman."

"Thank you, Aunt. I believe I will."

In the ensuing days, Elizabeth continued to meet with Mr. Darcy and his sister, both at the hospital and in other venues. Christmas was fast approaching, and with it, the spirit of the season seemed to take hold of them and, indeed, the entire city, as well. It seemed one could not pass another in the street without being greeted with a cheery "Happy Christmas!" or other such pleasantries. The shops began to show their Christmas wares, and everywhere there seemed to be joy and goodwill. Whether this was a product of Elizabeth's own heightened spirits, she decided not to question — the joy of the season was alive in her own heart, and that was enough.

The week after Mr. Darcy's return was also witness to an event, the resumption of an acquaintance Elizabeth who had not thought to see again. And while the meeting caused her pain initially, Elizabeth was able to find humor in it, and with the ineffable good cheer which had resided in her heart of late, she chose to hope for the future rather than regret the past.

On that day, Elizabeth had joined Mr. and Miss Darcy for a shopping trip. Not only had Elizabeth thought to purchase some small items for her mother and sisters for Christmas, but she also though to determine what she could possibly purchase for her new friends for Christmas. Of particular anxiety was what she could give to Mr. Darcy, for what did one give to a man to who possessed the means of purchasing anything he wanted whenever the fancy took hold of him? It was a conversation with Georgiana before they departed on their venture which taught Elizabeth a simple truth and proved her future sister was more perspicacious and wise than Elizabeth had imagined.

"My brother particularly likes books," replied Georgiana when Elizabeth asked her the question. "But I could not say what he has and what he still requires. I am not as much of a reader as William, though I do my share."

"A book might be acceptable," said Elizabeth, fretting just a little. "But it seems so . . . impersonal. I wish to gift your brother with something far more special than a simple book."

"You are thinking on this too much, Lizzy," replied Georgiana. "William will love whatever you see fit to gift him with, regardless of what it is."

"Oh?" asked Elizabeth. "Why do you say that?"

"Because it will be from *you*," replied Georgiana as if it was the most obvious thing in the world. She reached over and squeezed Elizabeth's hand. "As long as it is from your heart, Lizzy, William will love it."

The truth was so simple, yet so profound, and she could not say that Georgiana was incorrect. And with her friend's simple advice, Elizabeth knew exactly what she wanted to do for Mr. Darcy for Christmas. She smiled and thanked her friend and allowed the matter to drop. Georgiana seemed to sense that Elizabeth had come to some decision, for she looked on Elizabeth with curiosity written on her brow. But she did not ask, and Elizabeth did not offer any further information.

Another purpose for their excursion that day was to purchase some small gifts for the children at the hospital, for which Mr. Darcy had pledged for himself. Thus, they found themselves scouring Bond Street and beyond, debating this toy or that doll, slowly accumulating the items they meant to purchase for the children. As they gathered the various items together, they were purchased and stowed in the Darcy carriage, awaiting the shoppers.

The toy stores were not the only locations they visited, of course. They took some time at the bookstore, Elizabeth and Darcy debating their favorite authors and books, while Georgiana complained good-naturedly about obtaining a sister with such proclivities.

"I never thought I would find a woman who was as devoted to books as my brother," said she when they had been in the shop for some time.

"And yet, even my devotion to the written word pales in comparison with my father's," said Elizabeth, surprised for a moment that her father's absence did not bring the usual pang of sorrow. "Though his library was not large, the shelves positively groaned with the bounty he collected."

"A man after my own heart," said Mr. Darcy, approval evident in his tone. "I believe I would have liked to know your father."

"And he would have liked to know you, Mr. Darcy," replied Elizabeth. A wistful thought crossed her mind. "Unfortunately, Mr. Collins was not of a similar taste in books. I understand he sold all my father's books to line his pockets."

"I never would have guessed Mr. Collins would do that," was Mr. Darcy's dry response.

"Of course, I believe I had the last laugh in that exchange," said Elizabeth, her spirits reviving again. When her companions bestowed questioning glances on her, Elizabeth said: "Though he studies at the seminary, it was clear Mr. Collins had not much education otherwise. There were a number of my father's books which were first editions or rare copies. But Mr. Collins sold them in a bulk sale, not realizing that fact. I am certain he made only half the profit he might have otherwise."

"A fitting punishment," said Mr. Darcy with approval. "Though all he accomplished was to enrich the buyer more than he might otherwise have done."

"Mr. Russel is an old friend of my father's," said Elizabeth. "Likely because Papa bought so many books from him. I managed to save several of them before we left the neighborhood, and Mr. Russel even sold some few of the rarer books at a price much less than he otherwise might have been able to charge for them. He said it was the least he could do for all the patronage my father gave him over the years."

Again Mr. Darcy nodded in approval, and they continued their debate. They patronized several more shops that afternoon, including a few that only Georgiana and Elizabeth possessed any interest in. Mr. Darcy went along in good-natured agreement, never complaining, but always attentive, always ready to indulge the ladies in anything which gave them pleasure. Then they partook of tea and cakes at a small café not far from the bookshop, completing a wonderful day in one another's company.

When they quit the café, they wandered about for a short time, looking in the windows of shops they had not entered, speaking together in an animated fashion. At one point, Mr. Darcy indicated he wished to go inside one of the shops, and while Elizabeth might have gone in with him, a display in a window across the street caught her eye, and she turned to Mr. Darcy with a smile.

"I will wait here for you, Mr. Darcy."

Mr. Darcy noted the shop she intended to visit, and acknowledged her intention, informing her he would return in a short time. He then entered, Georgiana trailing along behind, leaving Elizabeth to herself. She crossed the road and stood outside the shop, looking at the wares in the window. The sun was shining that day, and while it was already well into December, she felt warmed by the light on her face and the pleasure of her experiences that day with her dearest friends. She was thus engaged when a voice reached Elizabeth's ears—a voice she recognized quite well and would have been happy to go without ever hearing again.

"Miss Eliza Bennet."

Turning, Elizabeth noted the presence of Miss Caroline Bingley, who stood there, looking down her nose at Elizabeth, that nose wrinkled as if some foul smell had wafted underneath it. She was dressed in her usually overdone fashion, a velvet gown of pale rose with a pelisse of deeper red over her dress, her headdress concocted of some impossibly large feathers. For a moment, Elizabeth was tempted to laugh, for she looked like a bird had taken up residence atop her head and built a nest.

"I thought it was you," continued Caroline with a superior sniff, one which conveyed a wealth of disdain. "Though I never would have thought *you*, of all people, would show your face in such a place as this, it seems that audacity is an essential part of your character."

"Caroline," said Elizabeth, choosing to ignore the other woman's tone. "The last I heard you were in York with the rest of your family."

While Caroline's eyes flashed in displeasure, accompanied by her glare, she maintained whatever composure she possessed. "It would be best if you did not refer to me by name, Miss Eliza. I have no wish to be associated with you."

Elizabeth suppressed a chuckle—should Caroline know with whom she was keeping company these days, Elizabeth had little doubt her manner would be completely different. Then again, she would almost certainly attempt to ingratiate herself with Mr. Darcy again.

"But we *are* connected, are we not?" observed Elizabeth, enjoying the anger her reminder provoked. "How have you been?"

"Do not attempt to claim an acquaintance," hissed Caroline. "Given your sister's infamous behavior, you have lost all right to any claim of society, even in that ridiculous little speck of a village in which you were raised. It is unfortunate I was not able to convince my brother to send that little baggage of a sister of yours away."

"Even *you* are not so senseless," rejoined Elizabeth. "Do you truly think your brother possesses the influence or wealth to actually divorce my sister?" Elizabeth smiled at the woman, a brittle sort of gesture she knew showed no warmth—not that she intended any. "Of course, given Charles married Jane because he loved her, I doubt any consideration would have induced him to send her away, as you assert."

"Do you think I have so little influence with my brother?"

"Your own words inform me of the paucity of the sway you have over him. Jane is still his wife and is not resident of some far-flung cottage in the fringes of Scotland, is she?"

Into this increasingly tense confrontation, Georgiana returned, apparently not realizing with whom Elizabeth spoke. "Lizzy, we shall depart in a moment."

As one, Elizabeth and Caroline turned, causing Georgiana to stop in surprise. Miss Bingley used her moment of shock to address her, turning a triumphant sneer on Elizabeth.

"Dearest Georgiana! Are you actually acquainted with Miss Eliza?"

"Yes, I am, Miss Bingley," said Georgiana. It could not be said she was slow of thought, as she peered at Caroline with something resembling trepidation. And well she should, for she likely understood as well as Elizabeth did herself how poorly Caroline would behave. The woman's next words proved Elizabeth's supposition.

"My friend," cooed she, stepping forward and taking Georgiana's arm, "I can see you have little knowledge of just what sort of woman you have allowed to impose upon you. But I can remedy that. Let us return to your brother's house, for I have information of which you — and your brother — should be aware."

"I am already well acquainted with Lizzy," said Georgiana, pulling her arm from Caroline's grasp. The older woman stumbled slightly, no doubt shocked by the manner in which Georgiana had rescued her captured limb. "There is nothing you can tell me about Lizzy that I do not already know."

"As I would have told you, had you not leaped to your erroneous conclusion," said Elizabeth, "I am here today with Georgiana. We shall be leaving together. Where is your party? Surely you did not come alone."

Caroline sniffed and glared at Elizabeth before once again drew close to Georgiana, though she did not attempt to grasp her arm again. "Perhaps you *think* you know Miss Eliza, but I am certain you know only what she has told you. Come away with me, my dear, and I shall explain all." Caroline favored her with what she considered to be a winsome smile, but which only appeared condescending. "You do not know what you are about, dearest Georgiana."

"First, Miss Bingley," said Georgiana, her firm tone obviously taking Caroline by surprise, "I have never given you leave to address me so informally. To you, I am Miss Darcy, if you please.

"Second, what I have heard from Elizabeth, *has* come directly from her. Given the tale she related to me and the pain it caused her, I have no doubt that every word is true. Now, if you will allow us to continue on our way, it would be much appreciated. We were about to depart for the carriage to return her to her uncle and aunt's house."

"Your uncle and aunt in *Cheapside*, is it?" sneered Caroline. "Of course! You are no longer the daughter of a gentleman, so you must subsist with those of lesser standing in the world. Not that your *father* was a true gentleman, after all, given his insignificant estate and your *mother's* less than stellar background."

Anger erupted in Elizabeth's breast at this stupid woman's brazen attack. Without considering the consequences of airing her family's dirty laundry on a public street, Elizabeth responded.

"Oh, my father was a gentleman. Eight generations of Bennet masters of Longbourn attest to that fact. And as for my mother, she is the daughter of a solicitor. But I suppose that the daughter of nothing more than a *tradesman* can have no understanding of the difference in standing between gentlemen, solicitors, and tradesmen, now can she?"

Outrage burned in Caroline's eyes, and she opened her mouth to retort. It was perhaps fortuitous that at that very moment, the missing members of both parties approached and interrupted the spat. A movement from behind Caroline caught Elizabeth's attention, and she saw Mr. and Mrs. Hurst hurrying toward them, and at the same moment, Mr. Darcy hailed them.

"Georgiana! Miss Bennet! I apologize for making you wait."

Focused as she was on Caroline, Elizabeth witnessed the woman's start of surprise as she caught sight of Mr. Darcy. Clearly, she seemed to have been of the opinion that Elizabeth had somehow managed to impose on Georgiana without Mr. Darcy's knowledge. Elizabeth also saw Caroline's eyes dart to her and noticed the wrinkles appear on her forehead and about her eyes as her scowl became even deeper.

"Hurst," said Mr. Darcy as he noticed their presence, his tone neutral. "I had no idea you were in town."

The grunt with which Mr. Hurst responded was nothing Elizabeth had never heard from the man. "Louisa and Caroline detest York, and they do not like my estate much better. I had much rather come to town than listen to their constant complaints."

Both women flushed at Mr. Hurst's blunt statement, but Miss Bingley was not about to be silenced. With another contemptuous glare at Elizabeth, she turned to address Mr. Darcy.

"It is fortunate you have come, Mr. Darcy, for it seems the standards of the society your sister keeps have fallen. Let us depart together, and I will explain to you exactly what manner of woman your sister has befriended."

"Your statement presupposes I do not already know."

Mr. Darcy's blunt statement hung in the air, Miss Bingley looking on him with unadulterated horror. She attempted to speak again, but Mr. Darcy did not allow it.

"Please allow me the benefit of my own understanding, Miss Bingley." He turned an affectionate eye on Elizabeth and grasped her hand, tucking it into the crook of his arm. "Georgiana and I are quite well acquainted with Miss Bennet, and we are both satisfied with her qualities. Besides, is it not the height of foolishness to attempt to cast a shade on Miss Bennet's character? After all, her sister is married to your brother. Any damage you do to her reputation will only redound upon your own, will it not?"

"As I have informed her more than once," said Mr. Hurst, looking at Caroline with considerable exasperation.

"My brother has declaimed all connection with the Bennets," snarled Caroline. "No one in town knows anything of them."

"I would prefer you did not take the chance," said Mr. Hurst. "If I am denied the sitting-rooms of our acquaintances in town because you have been imprudent, I will be very displeased. At that point, there will be no recourse but to return to the north."

Caroline understood his threat very well, for she turned away. "You know your brother has said you may not live with him, and if I do the same, your only option will be to return to the north and live with your maiden aunt. Or you could set up your own establishment with your dowry."

The scowl with which she regarded him did not daunt Mr. Hurst in the slightest, for he only returned her look with a blander one. Elizabeth was amused to note that it was Caroline who looked away first.

"Well, I am happy that is settled," said Mr. Hurst in a far more jovial tone than Elizabeth had ever heard. "It is good to see you again, Darcy. I hope we will be in each other's company again in the future."

"There is at present a rather large . . . impediment to that, Hurst," said Darcy.

It was not lost on anyone present that he referred to Caroline. The woman herself flushed even redder, and the glower she darted in Elizabeth's direction suggested she considered Elizabeth responsible for it. Elizabeth simply smiled, causing Caroline's look to become even darker if that was even possible.

"Yes, well, one of the reasons we are in town is for something to be done on that account," said Mr. Hurst. "If that outcome is not achieved, the options I mentioned before will become a reality — or at least one of them will."

Mr. Darcy nodded in perfect understanding of Mr. Hurst's meaning. "In that case, perhaps I shall see you at the club. Until then, we shall have to rely on such meetings to continue our acquaintance."

"Very well." Mr. Hurst turned to his two companions. "It is time for us to return to the house. Come along, Louisa, Caroline."

It seemed Caroline knew nothing of defeat, for she opened her mouth to speak again. This time her sister prevented whatever she was about to say.

"*Now*, Caroline."

This byplay had little effect on Mr. Darcy, for he turned away from the two ladies with Elizabeth on his arm, drawing Georgiana to him as well. They made their way back to the carriage largely in silence, each thinking upon the confrontation which had just taken place. But they waited until they had returned to the carriage before they began speaking of the matter—unlike the unwise Caroline Bingley, no one in the Darcy party wished to speak of such matters where they could be overheard.

When they were ensconced within, Mr. Darcy asked them about the confrontation, his countenance growing darker as first Elizabeth, then Georgiana, explained their perspectives of Miss Bingley's behavior. In the end, he could only shake his head.

"It is nothing more than I would have expected from Caroline," said Elizabeth, chuckling to inform them she had remained uninjured in the face of the woman's attacks. "She is as imprudent as ever, her view of herself as silly as it ever was."

"But you handled her marvelously, Lizzy," said Georgiana.

"As did you, my dear," replied Elizabeth. "I thought she would suffer apoplexy when you pulled your arm from her grasp, to say nothing of her shock when you instructed her to address you more formally."

Georgiana gave a little giggle. "I have wanted to do that for ages!"

"You shall not be forced to endure her again," said Mr. Darcy. "When next we meet, I shall remind Hurst that Miss Bingley is a persona non grata to the Darcy family."

"I am sure he already knows."

"Undoubtedly he does. But it appears Miss Bingley must be reminded."

By tacit agreement, the subject of Miss Bingley was dropped, and they turned to other topics. They spent the rest of the journey back to Gracechurch Street in lively conversation, and the matter of Elizabeth's unfortunate—though fortunately distant—relation's behavior was forgotten.

CHAPTER XI

$\mathcal{A}$cquainted with the woman as he was, Darcy fully expected Miss Caroline Bingley to make another attempt to lower Miss Bennet in his eyes. It was not so much her desire to be mistress of Pemberley which would push her along, though that was certainly a part of it—even a year and a half out of his company and the last words they had spoken would not be enough to diminish her misplaced confidence. Of more consequence to her way of thinking, however, was her pride, which would never allow her to acknowledge being bested by a woman she considered inferior.

The mere thought that Miss Bingley could consider herself superior to Miss Bennet in *any* way was unfathomable to Darcy. Miss Bennet was kind to all, while Miss Bingley was haughty and unpleasant; Miss Bennet loved working with the children at the hospital, while Miss Bingley, Darcy suspected, would not wish to be seen in such a place; Miss Bennet was pure, her beauty natural and unconstrained, while Miss Bingley was a woman given to primping and preening when in Darcy's opinion, she was barely tolerable in appearance. Furthermore, Georgiana loved Miss Bennet, while she detested the very sight of Miss Bingley. There truly was no comparison between them—Miss Bennet was superior in every way that mattered.

Ensconced in his study, Darcy leaned back in his chair, his work forgotten, a series of images of Miss Bennet rushing through his mind. Miss Bennet engaged in some errand at the hospital, cold morning air kissing her cheeks, making them rosy and bright, the sound of her laughter filling the world with light and joy, and perhaps the sight that had affected him the most, Miss Bennet sitting with the little girls at the hospital, giving of herself to help those less fortunate. For a man with marriage on his mind like Darcy, such a picture was a powerful insight of what might be, if he could only secure her as his wife. The thought of Pemberley filled with children laughing with their mother's voice almost spurred Darcy to go to Gracechurch Street that very instant and propose.

But he held himself back. There was no need to be precipitous, and Darcy knew it would be much more joyful for her if he simply adhered to his plan. That he was impatient was beyond dispute. But he would hold himself back, ensure that he acted in the manner he had already decided.

It was some thirty minutes later, after Darcy had once again forced his attention to his work, that the inevitable visit took place. A knock sounded on his door, and when Darcy gave permission to enter, the door opened, and Georgiana slipped into the room, a rueful grin set upon her countenance.

"Miss Bingley just arrived," said she without preamble. "As you predicted."

"Come, Georgiana," said Darcy with a smirk, "did you truly think she would not come to talk some sense into us?"

"*You*, you mean," said Georgiana with some disgust. "There is little chance she wishes me to be present."

"No, I am sure she does not. But I will not be in a room with that woman alone. Desperation induces a person to act without thought, and as Miss Bingley has rarely thought about anything other than her own selfish desires, I suspect she might be moved to try something underhanded."

A grin was Georgiana's response. "Then let us go into battle, Brother. Though I am not conversant with playing the role of a gallant knight, I shall have no difficulty in doing so if it prevents Mrs. Bingley's intrigues from being successful."

"I would never be induced to marry her, even if she did manage to compromise me," muttered Darcy.

His sister simply maintained her grin, waiting for Darcy to join her and offer his arm. While he would have preferred almost anything other than speaking again to Miss Bingley, Darcy knew it was best to allow the confrontation, so she may be ejected as soon as may be. Thus, he offered his arm to his sister and led her from the room. According to his instructions, Miss Bingley had been placed in a smaller parlor near the front of the house. The woman would likely feel offended at it, as the room was rather outdated in décor, and not suitable to visit with guests. Darcy hoped this was so—maybe if she *were* offended, she would feel some measure of his lack of regard for her. Not that he thought it was likely for her to be so self-aware.

When Darcy entered the room, nodding to the footman who was stationed there, he caught sight of Miss Bingley, who was pacing the length of the room in front of the fireplace, her expression telling the tale of her displeasure. She brightened when she saw him, but then she caught sight of Georgiana, and her eyes narrowed. It was impossible to deduce her intentions—or what intentions she might have possessed had Georgiana not been present—but her reaction told Darcy she had understood his reason for bringing his sister quite well, indeed.

"Mr. Darcy!" exclaimed she, clearly ignoring that which she did not like to acknowledge. "And dearest G—Miss Darcy. How lovely it is to see you again."

Out of the corner of his eye, Darcy could see his sister's effort to suppress her laughter at Miss Bingley's near slip. As it was, he was too impatient to get to the point of the conversation and be done with her to have any patience for pleasantries when he felt anything but pleasant.

"Miss Bingley," said he, his bow almost imperceptible. "How may we help you?"

Again, she noted his lack of enthusiasm and borderline insult, but other than a slight tightening around her eyes, she ignored it. "I had hoped to speak with you alone, Mr. Darcy." She smiled and batted her eyes, her coquettish simpering accomplishing nothing other than to fill him with revulsion. "While I am happy to visit with your lovely sister at any time, perhaps that may be accomplished after we speak."

"There will be no time—either now or in the future—when you will have occasion to speak with me alone, Miss Bingley." The smile ran away from Miss Bingley's face, and Darcy was astounded that she should be so confident, considering his behavior only the day before, not to mention eighteen months before at Pemberley. "Whatever you must say, please say it now or be done. I have much work I must accomplish today, for we are to dine with Miss Bennet and her family tonight."

That last was perhaps not necessary to say to Miss Bingley, but Darcy could not help himself. It seemed like Miss Bingley understood the point of his remark, for she scowled.

"It is precisely for this reason I have come," said Miss Bingley with a commendable attempt to rein in her temper. "Though I would never injure you, Mr. Darcy, by suggesting you are not in possession of the ability to choose with whom you associate, I am afraid your knowledge concerning Miss Eliza is sadly lacking. It is unfortunate you did not allow me to inform you yesterday. As a result, I have come today to be of use to you."

"You dishonor her, Miss Bingley," said Georgiana. "As her elder sister is married, her proper form of address is 'Miss Bennet.' Unless, of course, she has given you leave to address her by her Christian name."

"It matters little *how* you refer to her," snapped Miss Bingley, seemingly losing patience. "In no possible manner can she be considered a suitable acquaintance for one of your station."

"I shall make that judgment, Miss Bingley," said Darcy. "It would be very much appreciated if you would not attempt to usurp my authority."

"Has she bewitched you?" demanded Miss Bingley as she threw her hands up and resumed pacing. "There is no accounting for your blindness in this matter!"

"The only person she has bewitched is my brother," said Georgiana with a smile of amused satisfaction. "But I am certain Brother does not see that as a detriment. Quite the contrary, in fact."

"No," breathed Miss Bingley, her eyes widening in horror.

"Peace, Georgiana," said Darcy, wishing his sister would not taunt Miss Bingley in this matter. His sister did nothing more than beam at him and turn back to Miss Bingley, daring her to speak again. It was a dare Miss Bingley was only too willing to accept.

"Please, you must listen to me! There are such events in the history of the family of that little baggage as to render any sort of alliance with her impossible!"

"Are you, perhaps, referring to her sister falling to the sibilant whispering of a practiced deceiver?" asked Darcy.

Miss Bingley paled—clearly, she had thought that Elizabeth would endeavor to hide such a matter as her greatest secret. It was what Miss Bingley would have done in a similar situation, after all.

"You are already aware of it?" gasped she.

"Of course, we are," said Darcy, as Georgiana nodded by his side. "Miss Bennet told us of the matter herself, unable to support the idea that her friendship with us was formed under false pretenses. Did you truly think she would attempt to conceal it?"

That Miss Bingley thought exactly that was not a surprise. But she did not immediately respond.

"Lizzy would never do that," averred Georgiana. "Others might, but Lizzy's integrity is beyond question."

"That is singular behavior, indeed!" cried Miss Bingley, finally finding her tongue. "It is impossible to account for such willful disregard for all that is right and proper. Could it be possible that you, Mr. Darcy, a paragon of all that is right and virtuous, would be induced to forget everything you have been taught and consort with a woman who may bring about your downfall?"

Darcy was so incensed with Miss Bingley's tirade that he did not trust himself to respond. Georgiana was not affected in a manner similar and responded for them both.

"What has Elizabeth done which is so heinous, Miss Bingley? Of what can you accuse her?"

"She has a *sister* who is fallen," spat Miss Bingley. "I saw it all! A senseless mother who encouraged her daughters in their flirtatious behavior combined with an indifferent father, allowing their girls to abandon all delicacy and disgrace the entire family. Should she not be censured and despised?"

"Unlike some, I do not assign the blame for the misstep of one sister to all the others," said Georgiana. "Taint by association is one of the most disgusting things in our society. Furthermore, I am acquainted with Mr. Wickham's silver tongue and can only feel pity for Elizabeth's sister."

"Do you see?" demanded Miss Bingley, rounding on Darcy. "Do you not see how that upstart has poisoned your sister with her impertinent opinions?"

"Opinions with which I happen to agree."

Even at this late date, the woman was shocked at Darcy's words. Her confidence was something he could not fathom. Darcy had a significant amount of experience with those who believed only what they wished—Wickham was a prime example of such a trait. But he had never seen anyone as wilfully blind as Caroline Bingley.

"Let us come to the point, Miss Bingley," said Darcy. "It is clear why you have come today, and I must say the application of your displeasure was completely misjudged. Did I not make it clear yesterday that I was quite happy with Miss Bennet's acquaintance?

"Of course, I did," continued Darcy when the woman seemed unable to respond. "But you, in your arrogance, ignored everything we said in Miss Bennet's support. If it is not already clear, I will now inform you, so there are no misunderstandings, that your opinion is neither desired nor valued. The Darcy family will not end our acquaintance with Miss Bennet due to your displeasure.

"On the other hand, I have no desire to continue an acquaintance with you, regardless of the state of my friendship with your brother. For the moment, you have had your say, and I now require you to leave. Do not speak to us in society or return to this house, for you will not be acknowledged and will not be allowed entrance."

For a woman as prideful as Miss Bingley, his words were a blow, the likes of which she had never before experienced. But contrary to what he might have expected, Miss Bingley did not wilt or show any sign of how crushing his set down was to her conceit. Instead, she looked down her nose at them, sniffed, and stalked toward the door.

"I suggest you do nothing to spread tales of Miss Bennet," said Darcy before she could depart. "Not only would they adversely affect you as well, but she will have my full support against society. Do not test the extent of my social influence, Miss Bingley."

A scowl was the woman's final response. She flung the door open and stalked away, the sound of her footsteps clicking against the tiles fading away until the butler closed the door behind her.

When she was gone, Darcy shared a look and a mutually shaken head with his sister. "With any luck, she will be gone forever."

"It would not be Miss Bingley if she surrendered that easily," said Georgiana. "But perhaps we shall be very fortunate."

Though Darcy shared her sentiments, now was not the time to consider such a disagreeable subject. Therefore, Darcy excused himself to return to his study and finish his work for the day. When he arrived, he noted that the post had come while he was butting heads with Miss Bingley. With interest, Darcy shuffled through it, noting the presence of a letter he had been awaiting for some time. He opened it and read through it quickly, a wide grin coming over his countenance. Yes, it would be a very happy Christmas, indeed.

"Have I become a selfish being, Aunt?"

The question, which had been growing on Elizabeth's mind these past days, did not seem to take Mrs. Gardiner by surprise, though it had been spoken into a quiet room where there had been little conversation for some time. The parlor was empty except for the two women, as the children were above stairs with their governess, while Uncle Gardiner had gone to his warehouses for the day. For the entirety of the morning, Elizabeth had been at sixes and sevens, alternately picking at her embroidery, looking out the window at nothing in particular, or wandering about the sitting-room with no purpose in mind.

"Why do you ask, Lizzy?" was her aunt's response.

"I should think it would have been obvious."

Mrs. Gardiner smiled and shook her head. "Perhaps it is. But humor me anyway."

"This whole situation," said Elizabeth. "Here I am in London, enjoying Mr. Darcy's attention, in company with his sister, anticipating the approaching Christmas season and the joys and expectations accompanying them. Yet, my mother and two remaining sisters are trapped in a small cottage in Essex with little society and fewer funds. And yet, I have not thought of them much, especially these past weeks since Mr. Darcy came into my life."

"Was Jane selfish when she left for the north and left you all behind?"

"That is different, Aunt," replied Elizabeth with a frown. "Jane did not wish to leave us all behind—our tearful farewell informed me of that, had I not already known. But her husband decided it was best to protect his family from Lydia's scandal, and though I miss my sister dreadfully, I could not argue with his decision."

"But did Jane do anything to try to persuade him?" pressed Aunt Gardiner.

Elizabeth paused, not sure how to respond, allowing her aunt to continue. "Think on it, Lizzy. In my opinion, Mr. Bingley acted precipitously in this matter. Yes, the scandal had affected you in Meryton, but after your father's death and your family's departure from Meryton, the scandal was contained in that community. It seems to me unnecessary for Mr. Bingley to cut you all off so completely."

Frowning, Elizabeth considered her aunt's words. She had never thought of the matter in such terms. Anyone might have acted the same way, and no one would have gainsaid them. When she made this observation to her aunt, Mrs. Gardiner clucked and shook her head.

"I am well aware of what society would say on the matter. And, yes, I understand Mr. Bingley's reasons for acting as he did. But answer me this: could you imagine Mr. Darcy making the same choice in such a situation? Even now the threat of scandal, while remote, does exist. Yet he has decreed it to be insignificant."

"But it is different in Mr. Darcy's case," said Elizabeth. Though she agreed with her aunt that Mr. Darcy was much steadier of purpose than Mr. Bingley, her loyalty to the genial man who had made her sister happy demanded she speak in his defense. "The scandal is now an old one, whereas Mr. Bingley was forced to make his decision in trying circumstances."

"Lizzy," said Mrs. Gardiner, putting aside her sewing, "I am not attempting to besmirch Mr. Bingley's character. I simply point out that Mr. Darcy would not have made such a decision, in my opinion. Yes, he would have worked to allay the scandal and remove your family from its effects, but I doubt he would have severed all contact.

"Where this relates back to Jane is her response to her husband's decision. You and I both know Jane—she is incapable of thinking poorly of anyone, and in such a situation, she is so complying that I doubt she said anything to her husband in protest of his decision. Jane is self-effacing to a fault. But in some respects, you must say that her decision to refrain from trying to persuade her husband otherwise is a form of selfishness."

"Perhaps you are correct, Aunt," replied Elizabeth. "But I cannot blame her for it."

"Nor do I suggest you do."

Elizabeth's eyes narrowed, and she glared at her aunt, who was now openly grinning at her. "You have changed the subject."

The accusation did not disturb Mrs. Gardiner in the slightest. "I *expanded* the subject, Lizzy."

Struck as hilarious, Elizabeth could only laugh, in which she was joined by her aunt. She had her answer, Elizabeth supposed, though had she thought in advance she would have known that Mrs. Gardiner would never claim Elizabeth as selfish.

"In response to your original question," said Mrs. Gardiner, "I do not think you are selfish. The subject of your mother and sisters *has* been raised, has it not?"

"It was you who suggested it, as I recall." Elizabeth paused. "The matter did not even enter my mind until I received my mother's letter."

"No, I cannot dispute your recollection of events, Lizzy. But I think there are a few matters you have neglected to consider."

At Elizabeth's curious expression, Mrs. Gardiner smiled and beckoned her to sit on the sofa next to her. Elizabeth obliged and was happy when Mrs. Gardiner wrapped an arm around her shoulders and held her tight.

"In your present circumstances, you are not in a position to assist your mother, are you?"

Elizabeth made a face and nodded, releasing a burst of air from her lips. "That is true."

"As such," continued Mrs. Gardiner, "there was little to be gained from thinking on the matter constantly. It seems to me your consideration for your mother has been appropriate—you have not been devoid of all thought of your family, nor have you thought of them excessively. And you must remember that your mother's behavior, especially after Lydia's disgrace, was trying. I do not blame you for wishing to be away from her.

"There is one more thing you must consider: when you become Mrs. Darcy—as I am now convinced you will—you will gain much more ability to assist your family, even if your future husband was to refuse all his assistance, which, I am certain you would agree with me, he will not."

"No," whispered Elizabeth. "I cannot imagine Mr. Darcy declining to be of assistance to my family."

"Then do not allow yourself to be burdened by guilt. There is no reason for it. Instead, use that vaunted ability of yours to think of the past only as it gives you pleasure, and have hope for the future."

There was nothing to do but laugh in the face of her own words being used to cheer her, and Elizabeth did so without reservation. While she would continue to wonder if she had done all she could for her mother, there was no reason to dwell on the past. And the future did look rosy, indeed!

"Now," said Mrs. Gardiner, "if your maudlin display is at an end, I believe there are at least two rambunctious children upstairs who would like an outing to the park. And I dare say it would do you good too."

"It would be my pleasure," said Elizabeth. "I shall go directly."

During the flurry of preparations which followed, Elizabeth reflected that the support of kind and intelligent relations was priceless. Had she not had the Gardiners to assist, Elizabeth could not quite imagine how she might have coped.

CHAPTER XII

*D*arcy house was alive with festive spirit and good cheer, and it did Darcy's heart good to see his sister so devoted to decking its walls with greenery. Though the siblings had always celebrated Christmas together, even in years when it was only they two, neither had had much heart for surrounding themselves in such visible reminders of the season. The years when they had stayed with their relations, the décor was handled by Lady Matlock, who had her own ideas of how the house should be displayed for the season.

This year, however, due to certain circumstances, Georgiana had been positively adamant in declaring they could not leave their walls bare of adornment. As such, on this, the Friday preceding Christmas, the staff was out in force, cheerily going about their cleaning, hanging boughs of holly, balls of mistletoe in the main sitting-room, and many other bits of color besides. And over all of this activity, Georgiana presided like a conductor directing an orchestra. Even Mrs. Chambers, the housekeeper, did not presume to insert herself into the business.

"It does the heart good, does it not, Mr. Darcy?" said the woman when she noted Darcy watching his sister's efforts. "I have not seen Miss Darcy this animated in some time."

"Indeed, it has been missing from her character. She has grown too shy, too reticent over the years."

"The young miss has been good for her."

Darcy suppressed a smile. It was a poorly kept secret that he intended to offer for Miss Bennet—Mrs. Chambers had taken one look at her when she visited Georgiana and had immediately taken to her. It boded well for their future together, for Elizabeth had charmed all who met her as effortlessly as she took breath.

"Is it not wonderful, William?" asked Georgiana as she skipped up to him in her excitement. "The house has not been this cheerful since Mama's passing."

"It has not," agreed Darcy.

"I cannot wait until next year! It shall be so much fun?"

"Why do you say that?" asked Darcy, amused at her childish joy. "How can it be different from this year?"

"Because," said Georgiana in an exaggerated fashion, "next year, we will likely be at Pemberley. If this house looks wonderful with our Christmas decorations, just think of what Pemberley will be like!"

Mrs. Chambers smiled and moved away, though Darcy suspected she would not give up their company to Mrs. Reynolds and Pemberley without a fight. For Darcy, his imagination was caught by the thought of Elizabeth at Pemberley, the dearest place in the world. Together, she and Georgiana would likely have the stately home sparkling with beauty and merriment, to say nothing of how Elizabeth would enliven the place with nothing more than the force of her own incandescent character. And suddenly Darcy could hardly wait, himself.

"How are the preparations?" asked Darcy, forcing such fantasies to the back of his mind. "It has been long since we have had guests staying here."

"Everything is proceeding well, William," said Georgiana. "Mrs. Chambers keeps all the rooms clean, as you know. She assures me the house will be spotless, the beds soft, the linens clean, and the sitting-rooms as comfortable as she can make them."

"Not that I doubted her for a moment, but it is good to hear it. I dare say this Christmas will be the most important for our family in quite some time."

"Important?" asked Georgiana, her tone teasing, one of her eyebrows raised in a manner reminiscent of a teasing young woman of their acquaintance. "How could this year possibly be different from any other year has been?"

Darcy frowned at his sister. "I do not know that I like this impertinence with which you appear to have been infected of late,

Georgiana."

"Would you prefer I return to silence?" asked his sister.

"No, dearest," said Darcy, grasping her shoulder and pulling her slight frame against his. "In fact, I am pleased that you are livelier than you used to be."

Georgiana colored and looked away. "I have not changed in essentials, you know. It is Lizzy's influence which allows me to behave so with her and the Gardiners. My presentation is still a source of anxiety."

"Then it is well that you are not to come out this upcoming season. A year should assist in gaining experience and preparing yourself."

"And shall I have a sister to assist in preparing me for my coming out?" asked his sister with a sly smile.

"That is the impertinence of which I spoke," said Darcy.

Georgiana ignored him. "I hope you do plan to grant me such a boon brother, and I have the perfect candidate in mind. If you like, I shall reintroduce her to your acquaintance when the opportunity presents itself, for I believe you should consider making her an offer."

"So I am not already acquainted with this lady?" asked Darcy, playing along for the moment.

"Of course, you are! She is a wonderful woman, poised and confident, accomplished and capable, who possesses a kindness which is quite uncommon. I cannot imagine you would consider spurning her."

"And does this paragon have a name?"

"Of course, she does!" exclaimed Georgiana. "For who does not? I am sure you will be very happy with her, brother, and I know she cannot wait until the day she bears the name Caroline Darcy!"

A gay peal of laughter erupted from Georgiana's lips at his look of disgust, and she skipped away from him like the young girl she was, turning her attention back to the staff's attempts to decorate. Darcy could only shake his head—Miss Bennet was having quite an impact on his shy sister if she could tease him in such a way. While they had always been close, Georgiana had always treated him like a respected elder brother or, perhaps, even a father.

The more Darcy thought about it, the more being teased by a pair of lovely young ladies appealed to him. Christmas could not come soon enough for his tastes.

On the Saturday before Christmas, Elizabeth once again found herself in the company of the Darcy siblings on the way to the hospital for the day. This time, however, she was accompanied by her Aunt Gardiner who had consigned the care for her children to the governess that day.

"I would not have you think I am eager to leave my children behind," said Mrs. Gardiner as the carriage clattered through the streets of London. "But it is beneficial to spend time away from them on occasion." A smile at the other three in the carriage was followed by her statement: "You will understand when you have children of your own."

"And yet you are in a carriage with us," said Georgiana, "bound for a location where many children are waiting for you."

"That is true," said Mrs. Gardiner. "But the salient point is that they are not *my* children!"

The laughter produced by this statement was the most prominent in Mrs. Gardiner's case—as the only one among them who had children of her own, she was the only one who could truly understand. Elizabeth thought she understood Mrs. Gardiner's point after a fashion. After all, though Lydia was her sister, rather than a daughter, there had been many times when Elizabeth would have gladly have dispensed with her silly and immature sister rather than enduring embarrassment on an almost continual basis.

For the first time in many months, the thought of Lydia brought a pang of sorrow to Elizabeth's breast, rather than the indignation which usually accompanied such reminiscences. Lydia had, by her behavior, caused much upheaval in her family, indirectly leading to her father's death. But she was still Elizabeth's sister, and whatever else happened, Elizabeth hoped her sister was well and happy wherever she was now.

"We shall have to take your word for it, Mrs. Gardiner," said Georgiana with evident amusement. "It shall be some time before I am in any position to verify the content of your words."

"Dear Georgiana," said Mrs. Gardiner, "it *should* be some time before you are in such a position, as you are yet young, and there is much a young lady has the freedom to enjoy before she is married. For *some* of the company," Mrs. Gardiner's gaze swept from Darcy to Elizabeth, "the possibility of children might be closer than you think."

Georgiana put a hand over her mouth and giggled while Elizabeth felt her cheeks heat. For Mr. Darcy's part, he did nothing more than smile and watch them all with considerable amusement. Hateful man! The least he could do was *pretend* to be embarrassed by their teasing.

"But perhaps it would be best to be silent," said Mrs. Gardiner. "I can see my niece piercing me through me with her eyes, and I suspect I will pay dearly for my teasing later tonight."

"You know me well, Aunt," said Elizabeth, her flat tone not affecting her aunt in the slightest.

In this lively manner, they passed the time until the carriage pulled into the courtyard before the hospital. When it pulled to a stop, Mr. Darcy descended and gallantly offered his hand to assist the ladies from the conveyance. Once inside, they doffed their outerwear and made their way as a group to where the children were awaiting their arrival. As had often become the case, the young girls, in particular, were delighted to see Elizabeth, and several approached her, though with some reserve and under the watchful eye of the matron.

"Miss Bennet," said Genevieve, the first to reach her. "We are so happy to see you today!"

"As am I to see you," said Elizabeth, crouching down to greet the girl. "You have behaved yourself since the last time I was here?"

The girl, along with several others near her, nodded vigorously. "Mrs. Mason informed us that Father Christmas will not visit us if do not behave ourselves."

"Mrs. Mason is very wise," said Elizabeth. "But I am sure he will come for such well-behaved young ladies as all of you."

The group of girls beamed at Elizabeth's words, and as a group, holding a pair of the cherubs' hands, they made their way toward the hall in which the residents of the orphanage gathered, for today was to be a special treat. The hall was to be decorated that day, with the help of the assistants who gave of their time. In addition to Elizabeth's party were several others whom Elizabeth had met at sundry times in the past weeks, but also Miss Howard and Lady Frances, who stood apart from the rest with sour countenances and whispered comments.

With the gathering complete, they began to place the ornaments about the hall. Mr. Darcy, with his height, began to hang streamers made of brightly colored paper along the walls, with the help of several other gentlemen. The ladies took boughs of holly and other greenery which had been gathered for the purpose, hanging them from the tables, hanging wreaths from the doors.

Throughout the hall, the excited chatter of the children added to the gaiety of the season. Elizabeth found her heart full, for these poor children, alone in the world, were being given a Christmas like any other child living with their parents. Genevieve, in particular, seemed unwilling to separate herself from Elizabeth's side. Happy to be of use to the small child, Elizabeth allowed her to stay close, lifting her up to help with the placement of the various items, allowing the child to feel the warmth of her love.

When the decking of the hall was completed, the company stood back and surveyed their work, many of the children clapping with delight and glee. The work done for the day, the matron called for the kitchens to provide refreshment for them all. When produced, their refreshments were brought, again causing gasps of surprise from the children when it was revealed to be crunchy gingerbread, coupled with cups of hot chocolate. Most of those children had likely never seen hot chocolate—Elizabeth herself had had it only once or twice—and their approbation was evident in the pleasure in which they talked and laughed as they partook of their sweet treats.

"It is strange, is it not, Mr. Darcy?" asked Elizabeth with her cup in her hand as she stepped close to him.

"What is strange, Miss Bennet?" asked Mr. Darcy.

"That an orphanage can afford to serve hot chocolate to the children, even on such a special occasion as this. They must have some wealthy patron who is generous enough to give them this small bit of pleasure."

Mr. Darcy looked at her from above his cup as he took a sip of his drink. "I believe they must, for this is excellent."

Though they were both aware that Elizabeth knew *exactly* from whence this largesse had sprung, Mr. Darcy refused to say anything more. Elizabeth allowed him to keep his secret, contenting herself with nothing more than a softly spoken: "Well done, Mr. Darcy. Well done, indeed."

One of the girls ran up to her at the moment and pulled her away to a table where a number of them sat together, and Elizabeth allowed herself to be led away. She did notice, however, the looks of outright disdain she was receiving from Miss Howard and Lady Frances, as she did the way the earl's daughter sidled over to Mr. Darcy and began speaking to him. Contrary to her designs, however, Elizabeth noticed that Mr. Darcy's features assumed an expression of distant indifference, which she knew he donned when uncomfortable. Elizabeth shook her head and turned her attention to the young girls, knowing that Mr. Darcy was not affected in the slightest by the haughty woman.

When their treat was consumed, the matron's assistants produced supplies of colored paper and pencils, and the children began to work on their little pictures and crafts. Elizabeth helped several of the little girls as they worked on their drawings, while some of the other girls folded their paper and used scissors to cut out bits of paper, which when unfolded, revealed themselves to be snowflakes of all shapes and colors. These were then taken and hung from the ceiling above them, adding to the merry nature of the scene.

When finally this was complete, the company adjourned to another room, wherein sat a pianoforte—an older piece, but still serviceable. There they sat with the children, singing Christmas carols together. A large Bible was produced, and Mr. Darcy was drafted to read the manger story. Then finally, at the end of the evening, some of the young ladies returned to the pianoforte to play for the children.

Among these was Lady Frances who Elizabeth was forced to confess possessed considerable ability at the instrument. Unfortunately, Elizabeth thought she had the same flaw that Miss Bingley possessed—rather than play the songs for the enjoyment of all, she seemed intent upon showing the extent of her talent, adding little trills and arpeggios when they were not required. The company applauded her performance, but it was by no means the most capital performance of the day.

After a time, Elizabeth rose to take her turn, but instead of sitting at the instrument, Georgiana took the bench and played while Elizabeth sang an old favorite of hers, While Shepherds Watched Their Flocks, to the approbation of the company. Then Georgiana began to play God Rest Ye Merry Gentlemen, and Elizabeth began to sing. But she was surprised when Mr. Darcy rose and strode to her side, singing along with her.

Never having heard him sing before, Elizabeth almost melted at the sound of his rich baritone weaving expertly with her mezzo-soprano. To Elizabeth's love-filled eyes, it seemed like he was singing directly to and for her, though the song was a well-loved, old Christmas hymn. The song ended with "O tidings of comfort and joy!" leading to the company clapping enthusiastically in response.

Elizabeth turned and smiled widely at Mr. Darcy, ignoring the approbation of the company. "You did not inform me you could sing with such skill, Mr. Darcy."

"That is because I rarely choose to display my talents, Miss Bennet. But seeing you singing, it looked very much like an angel had descended to grace us with her song, and I could not help myself." He leaned forward and said in a low voice: "Georgiana demanded I practice the song with her when she played, insisting that I stand up with you. It had been on my mind to refuse, but I could not resist. I dare say, I have made my sister very happy."

The look in his eyes, the tenderness with which he regarded her, the softness of his voice, filled Elizabeth with contentment such as she had never before felt. For perhaps the first time when he spoke to her in such a manner, Elizabeth felt no embarrassment at his attentions. She was suffused with nothing more than pleasure and love for him."

Somehow her hand found its way into his grasp, and Mr. Darcy seemed unwilling to remove it, though she was aware he most certainly should. But they stood there for what seemed like an eternity, staring into each other's eyes as if they were the only ones in the room.

"Miss Bennet! Miss Bennet!" said Genevieve as she again rushed up to them. "Can you teach me to sing?"

"Perhaps, Genevieve," said Elizabeth, again crouching down to speak to the child. "But you already sing beautifully. I dare say you will become even more accomplished as you grow."

The girl beamed at Elizabeth and then, looking back and forth between Elizabeth and Mr. Darcy said: "Shall you marry Mr. Darcy, Miss Bennet? I think you should?"

A snort escaped the gentleman's lips, informing Elizabeth of the gentleman's amusement. For her part, Elizabeth again felt her heart overflowing, and not at all disconcerted to know her affection for the gentleman was discerned by a mere child.

"If I am to marry Miss Bennet, Miss Genevieve," said Mr. Darcy, "you shall be the first to know. Would you like that?"

Genevieve nodded her head so vigorously that Elizabeth thought it might come loose. The assistants then began to gather the children together, for the day's events had come to a close and their supper time was approaching. When she saw their time was about to end, Genevieve threw herself into Elizabeth's arms, planting a large, wet kiss on her cheek.

"Thank you for coming today, Miss Bennet," said she in a voice which was credibly composed. "Shall we see you again before Christmas?"

"I believe you shall, Genevieve, my dear. And perhaps I might even visit you on Christmas itself. After all, I should like to be here when Father Christmas comes."

With a grin, Genevieve gave her another kiss and departed with the other children, waving at Elizabeth as she left. Elizabeth felt, rather than saw, Georgiana and her aunt join them to watch as the children were escorted away.

"It seems you have gained a friend for life, Lizzy," said Mrs. Gardiner.

"She is a dear child," replied Elizabeth. "They are all dear children." Elizabeth turned to her aunt. "I am so happy you have introduced me to the hospital, Aunt. It has been a wonderful experience to help these children."

"You are welcome, Lizzy," said Mrs. Gardiner. "But it is your open and affectionate heart which has gained you such blessings. Had you bemoaned your fate and looked inward instead of outward, this happiness would not now be yours."

Elizabeth understood all her aunt was saying, though Mrs. Gardiner refrained from looking at either of the Darcys. In response, she only drew her aunt into an embrace, a physical thanks for the equally large heart of her Gardiner relations, who had taken her into their hearts and home when she had most needed an escape.

"I cannot but agree with your aunt, Miss Bennet," said Mr. Darcy. "Not everyone could be what you have become to these children. You are truly a wonder."

Turning to look at the gentleman who had become so dear, Elizabeth stated: "No more than you, sir—or your lovely sister." Georgiana smiled at Elizabeth's praise and took her hand. "I believe there is enough praise to go around. There is no need to concentrate it on me."

The group began to make their way to the entrance, as the time had come to return to their homes. As they walked, Elizabeth continued to think about the children here. Although they had helped make the day and the season brighter for them, the fact remained that they were still orphans, still alone in the world. Elizabeth could not help but wish there was more that could be done for them, a fact she voiced to her companions.

"Perhaps there is more that can be done," said Mr. Darcy. "As they grow, positions could be found for them, to assist them in making their way in the world. I also know of several families in Derbyshire who may be willing to take children into their homes. One or two tenant families among Pemberley's tenants may be able to take a child into their home. It would not be an easy life, for a tenant must work for his livelihood, but it would certainly give them opportunities they might not otherwise have."

"That sounds wonderful, Mr. Darcy," said Elizabeth, looking up at the gentleman, admiring him for his thoughtfulness. "I have several friends in Hertfordshire with whom I am still in contact—there may be some families in Hertfordshire who could also accept children."

"Perhaps the process should be formalized," suggested Mrs. Gardiner. "There are undoubtedly families from all situations in life who would be blessed by the addition of a child to their midst."

"But they would need to be investigated to ensure they would treat a child as the precious gift they are." Elizabeth fell silent, her mind awhirl with possibilities. Though she had grown fond of these children and enjoyed spending time with them, a more long-lasting assistance would be to see them situated as her aunt suggested.

"That is a conversation for another day," said Mr. Darcy, "though I agree with you. For now, I believe we should depart."

They all agreed and the next several moments were spent donning coats and pelisses, scarves and gloves to protect against the elements outside. It was while Elizabeth was thus engaged when the only objectionable event of the day occurred. For Lady Frances sidled near to her when Mr. Darcy's back was turned and fixed her with a baleful glare.

"Do not believe your ambition will ever be gratified, Miss Bennet. Mr. Darcy has too much pride to offer for a penniless girl such as you." Lady Frances eyed her from head to toe, her lip curled in disgust. "He can do so much better than you."

"Whether he can or not is none of your concern."

The woman jumped at the sound of Mr. Darcy's severe voice behind her. But before she could form a response, Mr. Darcy gave her a clipped nod and stepped to Elizabeth, extending his arm for her to take.

"Shall we, Miss Bennet?"

"Thank you, Mr. Darcy," said Elizabeth, taking his arm.

It was a measure of Elizabeth's restraint that she did not glance back at Lady Frances as Mr. Darcy led her from the building. Though she could well imagine the woman's countenance at Mr. Darcy's dismissal, Elizabeth had no interest in seeing it for herself. Her attention was much too agreeably engaged to focus on a woman so full of herself as Lady Frances Graves.

Chapter XIII

*C*hristmas Day was fast approaching, and with it, Elizabeth found her anticipation heightening as if she were a child of five. There was something strange but wonderful occurring before her very eyes, something she could not quite put her finger on. There was nothing specific to point to it, but in certain circumstances and certain times, Mr. Darcy particularly had become secretive. Whether he had planned something for her, she did not know—the thought of a proposal caused her heart to pound within her chest—but the intelligent woman in Elizabeth told her something was happening of what she had not been told.

All of these thoughts flew from her mind, however, only three days before Christmas. On that particular day, Elizabeth had been engaged to visit Georgiana at Darcy house, but when she arrived there, she was to be confronted by a rather large surprise.

Having prepared to depart after breakfast that morning, Elizabeth descended to the breakfast room, where her aunt and uncle, already having broken their fast, we sharing a companionable cup of tea. Their warm greetings as Elizabeth entered were a contrast to the soft conversation Elizabeth was certain she was interrupting, but as they did not appear to have been sharing anything other than soft words of affection common between couples, she took no notice of it.

"Are you certain you do not wish to accompany me to visit Georgiana?" asked Elizabeth as she helped herself to some tea and a scone. "I am certain she would be vastly pleased to see you."

"No doubt she would," replied her aunt. "But we are to go there on Christmas, and I have many things I must do today. I am afraid you will need to go yourself, Lizzy."

"Very good of Mr. Darcy to invite the children too," said Mr. Gardiner. His lips curled with amusement. "Then again, I suppose Darcy understand that if he is to have *us*, he must suffer our children at the same time!"

"This account of Mr. Darcy is not at all accurate, Uncle," protested Elizabeth, though in a teasing tone. "To hear you speak, the man intends to suffer their presence in silence."

"And I hardly think he would suffer our presence if he truly did not enjoy our children," said Mrs. Gardiner. "Lizzy, on the other hand . . . ."

"Had I any notion you were in any way serious, I might take offense," said Elizabeth while calmly sipping from her teacup. "As it is, I know you like Mr. Darcy and his sister very well, and I am well aware you have seen him with the children as much as I have."

"Oh, aye," said Mrs. Gardiner, a teasing twinkle still shining in her eye. "I dare say Mr. Darcy will make an excellent father someday. Now he only requires a wife to assist him in *becoming* a father."

Mr. Gardiner guffawed at his wife's joke, but Elizabeth was by now largely inured to their teasing, not to mention secure in Mr. Darcy's affections. As such, she only smiled and nodded at her relations, saying: "Indeed. Perhaps he will choose a wife soon."

"I have no doubt he will," replied Aunt Gardiner.

"Very well, then," said Mr. Gardiner, rising to his feet. "Unfortunately, the needs of business do not disappear during the Christmas season, and, therefore, I should make my way to my warehouses."

Kissing his wife's and niece's foreheads in farewell, Mr. Gardiner nevertheless paused before leaving, fixing an amused smile on Elizabeth. "You are bound for Mr. Darcy's house this morning, as I recall. Shall I call for the carriage on my way out?"

"It is still too early, Uncle," said Elizabeth.

"Very well," replied he. "It seems to me that you have used my carriage much more than I have myself, of late. Just like a young woman, always flitting here and there without any thought to what my poor driver must suffer. Especially when Jacobs has been rather out of sorts since the break in the carriage wheel, not to mention how you abandoned him in favor of a church!"

Though knowing he was teasing, Elizabeth had harbored these thoughts herself of late. As such, she could not help but offer to simply take a hackney to Mr. Darcy's house.

"You will do no such thing," said Mr. Gardiner, his tone mock-severe. "It does my heart good to see you so happy when it was only recently that you were mired in depression. My carriage will often sit for some time, with my warehouses so close, and it does the team — and Jacobs! — good to get out on a more regular basis.

"Besides," continued he with a wink, "we would not want a family as prominent as the Darcys to think we are too poor to afford to send out the carriage whenever you visit."

With those final words, Mr. Gardiner said his farewells again and departed. Elizabeth watched him go, fondly thinking how his final words were ones her mother might have uttered. Of course, he said them with a lot more sense than her mother had ever possessed, and Elizabeth was not embarrassed by them like she often was when her mother opened her mouth to speak.

The rest of her time before she must leave was spent in companionable conversation with Mrs. Gardiner. After breakfast, they adjourned to the parlor, where Elizabeth assisted her aunt in her sewing, though she did not possess much skill. The third time she found her mind wandering along with her stitches, Mrs. Gardiner laughed and pulled the sewing away from her, shooing her from the house.

"It is now an acceptable time to visit, Lizzy," said Mrs. Gardiner, "and I am sure Georgiana will be waiting for you. If you continue on in such a fashion, those pants will have only one leg, and my eldest son will wonder *who* sewed them. Be gone with you!"

Eager as she was to be gone, Elizabeth agreed and left with alacrity. The carriage ride to the Mayfair district was uneventful, and Elizabeth was soon to be found climbing the stairs to Mr. Darcy's home. It was with more than a little surprise that Elizabeth noted Georgiana was not on the front steps of the house to greet her as was her usual wont. It was even more surprising to find that the Darcys were not alone. With them was an elderly woman of an obviously imperious nature.

"So, this is the young woman with whom you propose to supplant my Anne," observed the woman in a ringing and forceful tone.

For a moment, Elizabeth was not certain what to do. The lady sat in a chair at the end of the table in between two sofas, her eyes boring into Elizabeth, making her feel quite uncomfortable. She was quite tall, Elizabeth thought, her hair tied in a severe knot behind her head, now more gray than what must have been a silky black in her youth. Her eyes were a clear cerulean, a striking feature set in a long face which might have been handsome once. Her voice was, as Elizabeth had noted, loud and piercing, and she suspected the lady would have been more than capable of using it to great effect when someone crossed her wishes. Mr. Darcy and Georgiana sat on either side of her on the edges of the two sofas—though Mr. Darcy had risen upon Elizabeth's entrance—Georgiana looking utterly terrified, while Mr. Darcy's mouth was set in a firm line. His glance at her suggested apology, as if he would have preferred to spare her this ordeal. Given the circumstance, Elizabeth thought she knew exactly who this woman was.

"Well, Darcy," snapped the lady, her eyes flicking to her nephew, "do not stand there as if you are bereft of wit. It is well that she has come, for it saves me the trouble of sending for her. Since you have perpetrated this farce on the family, by all means—introduce us."

The muscles of Mr. Darcy's jaw clenched, and while Elizabeth might have thought he would refuse such an imperious request, he nevertheless approached Elizabeth. The tight smile he directed at her suggested solidarity and seemed designed to bolster her courage. And then in a sign even more blatant to the waiting lady, he tucked Elizabeth's hand in the crook of his arm, laying his free hand over hers, and turned to face his aunt. It was clear Lady Catherine was well aware of the meaning of this action.

"I would be happy to introduce you. Lady Catherine, this is Miss Elizabeth Bennet, formerly of Hertfordshire, now staying with her aunt and uncle on Gracechurch Street here in town. Miss Bennet, this is my aunt, Lady Catherine de Bourgh, of Rosings Park in Kent. Lady Catherine is my late mother's sister.

Elizabeth curtseyed to the lady, who barely deigned an incline of her head in response. Determined to make the best possible impression on this woman, Elizabeth rose from her curtsey and addressed her ladyship.

"I am pleased to make your acquaintance, Lady Catherine. I hope your journey from Kent was comfortable."

"Until we invent a new means of travel," said Lady Catherine, "I doubt *any* journey will be comfortable. But it was tolerable, I suppose."

The first comments exchanged, Mr. Darcy led Elizabeth to the sofa on which he sat before, situating himself in the location he had occupied while seating Elizabeth to his side away from Lady Catherine. Clearly, Lady Catherine understood the significance of this placement as well, for she scowled at her nephew. The look he returned was bland, though with a hint of challenge. Lady Catherine did not rise to it.

"It seems to me I have heard the name Bennet before, Miss Bennet, and equally clear you are not unfamiliar with my name. Might I ask you to elucidate on the specifics of our connection? Present company excluded, of course."

"There was a clergyman in your employ some time ago by the name of Mr. Collins," said Elizabeth. The way her ladyship looked at her, Elizabeth was certain Lady Catherine was already well aware of the connection. "Mr. Collins is my late father's cousin, and has inherited his estate."

"Yes, I remember Mr. Collins very well, indeed." Lady Catherine paused, seeming to consider her words. "It seems I may have . . . misjudged my actions with Mr. Collins to a certain extent."

At Elizabeth's curious glance, her ladyship said: "Having met the man, I assume you are well aware of his . . . limitations?"

Though the urge to laugh was strong, Elizabeth stifled it and conceded that she was.

"Then you know that he is not the most intelligent of men. While I was well aware of his veneration for me—a useful tool at times, though a bother more often—I was not aware of the extent of his attachment until he departed to take up his inheritance." Lady Catherine huffed with annoyance. "The man could not make a single decision without writing me a four-page letter—ones which could have been shortened to a paragraph and still conveyed what was necessary.

"Fortunately, it seems I have had success lately in transferring his never-ending questions to his wife, for he has not written to me in three weeks."

"That is good news," said Elizabeth. "Charlotte is a sensible woman. With her guiding him, I have no doubt Longbourn will be a successful estate."

"Yes, well, I hope so. I have enough to do to care for my own estate without being required to answer Mr. Collins's letters on a daily basis."

"I trust you have found a replacement for him?" interjected Mr. Darcy.

Lady Catherine seemed annoyed at his interruption, but she

confirmed his question readily. "Mr. Rogers is by no means as obliging as Mr. Collins," said she. "But in some ways that is well, for I need not be so attentive to his doings."

Again Elizabeth suppressed a snicker. Her acquaintance with the gentleman told her that Mr. Collins likely required guidance every minute of every day, lest he make a hash of the parish's business. Elizabeth doubted he would be any more competent when it came to managing an estate. Lady Catherine might have enjoyed a sycophant hanging off her every word, eager to do her every bidding, but Elizabeth thought it might have become tiring after a time, even if one was of a disposition to enjoy such continual praise.

"Might I assume," continued the lady, "that *you* are the Bennet sister who so foolishly rejected Mr. Collins's offer of marriage?"

"I am," replied Elizabeth. "It is a matter of perspective, I suppose, as to whether it was foolish."

"How so, Miss Bennet?" Lady Catherine's eye bored into Elizabeth, and she seemed to be daring Elizabeth to say anything which might contradict Lady Catherine's expected opinions. It was fortunate—for Elizabeth—that she was well able to speak for herself and ignore any of Lady Catherine's attempts at intimidation.

"If one considers matters of situation alone, I suppose my refusal might appear imprudent. However, I take pride in knowing myself, Lady Catherine. My short acquaintance with Mr. Collins informed me that I would be miserable with him as a wife, and I have no doubt *he* would be equally miserable with me."

"You would be miserable with a home of your own? Is there not more misery in being a burden on your aunt and uncle?"

"My aunt and uncle have assured me repeatedly that I am not a burden."

"Miss Bennet," said Lady Catherine, closing her eyes in frustration, before opening them and peering at Elizabeth again. "I would ask you to be serious and frank with me, for I am no less."

"Perhaps I was a little flippant in my answer," said Elizabeth. "But I assure you, Lady Catherine, that I am aware enough to know how I would fare in a marriage with the likes of Mr. Collins. My friend, Charlotte, possesses the patience to endure him, and perhaps more importantly, always wished for nothing more than a home and situation of her own."

Elizabeth paused and smiled at a sudden memory. "In fact, Charlotte once told me she thought it was best to know as little as possible of the defects of one's partner in advance.

"I, however, require more in a marriage than what which my friend sought. While I know you will likely scoff at my assertion, I wish for love in any partnership." Elizabeth paused and looked Mr. Darcy, struck with the tender look he directed at her. It was incumbent upon Elizabeth to continue before she was distracted by the reality of Mr. Darcy's close presence. "If I cannot have love, then I wish for respect at the very least. The fact that I could neither love nor respect Mr. Collins formed a serious impediment to my future happiness if I should be foolish enough to accept him."

It seemed to Elizabeth that Lady Catherine looked on her with, perhaps, a little more respect than she had before. It did not seem that respect, if it actually did exist, was enough to allow the lady a little less severity of manner, for when she spoke again, the accusing note in her voice was still present.

"It is not my purpose to argue regarding your actions with respect to Mr. Collins, Miss Bennet. Many would say your refusal of a man who could provide for you and your family was, indeed, reckless. However, you seem to have considered the matter at length. While I cannot, in general, agree that such imprudent decisions are correct and just, I cannot accuse you of rejecting my former parson without due consideration."

"Thank you, Lady Catherine," said Elizabeth, and try as she might, she could not keep a hint of a wry quality from her voice.

"I will ask you not to be snide," said Lady Catherine. "Perhaps you do not know, Miss Bennet, but this match to which you aspire is not only unequal in the extreme—a circumstance you point out yourself as being unwise—but there is a prior claim on my nephew. Now, tell me what you have to say about that."

"Lady Catherine—" interrupted Darcy, but Lady Catherine interjected before he could continue.

"Be silent, Nephew. Do you doubt Miss Bennet's ability to reply? I wish to hear from her—you may speak later."

"I am perfectly willing to respond, Mr. Darcy," added Elizabeth.

The concern with which he regarded her spoke to his serious reservations concerning the matter. For her part, Elizabeth was confused at the lady's actions thus far. From everything she had heard from first Mr. Collins, in addition to the comments Mr. Darcy had made these past weeks, she might have thought the lady would blow in like a gale, snapping and snarling at all in her path, demanding she be obliged. Though she was forceful and demanding, Elizabeth had not found the lady to be as bad as she thought she might.

Finally, Mr. Darcy subsided, though the creases in his brow continued to speak to his concern. But he did not attempt to interrupt again. Thus, Elizabeth essayed to make her response.

"Of the specifics, I, of course, cannot speak," said Elizabeth to Lady Catherine. "Mr. Darcy has spoken of an agreement between you and your sister concerning himself and your daughter."

"Then you acknowledge it?" said Lady Catherine.

Elizabeth regarded the lady, wondering what game she was playing. Again, the question, though forceful, did not hint to a smugness Elizabeth might have expected in such a circumstance. Instead, it felt like Lady Catherine was attempting to test her, to see for herself what measure of mettle Elizabeth possessed.

"Again, I will stress that I have only heard from Mr. Darcy," replied Elizabeth. "But he is of the opinion that he is not bound by your agreement."

"As I have told you myself," said Mr. Darcy.

The lady huffed at her nephew's interruption and fixed her attention on Elizabeth once again. "I am well aware of my nephew's recalcitrance. What I wish to know is how you have the audacity to imagine yourself fit to stand in the place my sister once stood. Do you think so well of yourself as to imagine you are equal to a woman of such quality?"

"I imagine myself capable of whatever Mr. Darcy requires in a wife," was Elizabeth's pointed reply. "I do not presume to be the equal of your sister, nor do I think I am taking her place. I am a young woman, Lady Catherine. It is beyond doubt that I possess weaknesses aplenty. But I trust anything I lack to not include those of understanding or ability."

"Yes, well, I must confess you do not lack in confidence," said Lady Catherine in a tone of grudging respect. "But what of your breeding? Your father was a gentleman, it is true, but I am well aware that your mother's line is not so illustrious. How do you intend to live up to the standards of a Darcy in society?"

"Forgive me for saying it, Lady Catherine," said Elizabeth, "but I do not consider my breeding to be an impediment. Should Mr. Darcy offer for me, he would be marrying me—not my family."

"For a young woman who speaks so well, it seems you are ignorant in the ways of the world. Do you not know that your family will reflect upon my nephew?"

"I am well aware of it. But my family will not always be among us."

"But they will be at times."

"Perhaps."

"And what of your youngest sister?" Elizabeth frowned at the lady, who huffed. "Do not think you can intimidate *me*, Miss Bennet. Yes, I am aware of your youngest sister's actions, including your father's demise. Given what you know of Mr. Collins, can you think he did not relish to relate the matter to me in full? Is this sister to be invited to Pemberley, to cavort in the halls of that venerable estate, when she has been involved with such a reprehensible creature as the son of my brother's former steward?"

"That is quite impossible, Lady Catherine," said Mr. Darcy quietly. All eyes swung to him—even Georgiana, for whom Mr. Wickham was at times a touchy subject, looked at her brother with interest.

"Miss Lydia has left these shores, never to return," said Mr. Darcy. Elizabeth was shocked, and Mr. Darcy, seeing this was quick to explain. "I hired a man to look into her situation, Miss Bennet, for while I knew you still loved her as your sister, I suspected you would not wish to meet with her again."

"That is true," said Elizabeth, albeit reluctantly. "Did you send her away?"

"No," replied Mr. Darcy. "My investigator followed the trail of her movements and learned that she and a Lieutenant Denny departed from England to try their luck in the New World. She had left England within three months of disappearing from your mother's cottage." Mr. Darcy paused and gave Elizabeth a wan smile. "I meant to tell you, Miss Bennet, though in less fraught circumstances. The investigator did not follow her trail across the ocean, as it would be expensive and difficult. But I wished you to at least have this certainty about your sister's fate."

"And I thank you, Mr. Darcy," said Elizabeth, reaching out and placing a hand on his arm. "It is for the best that Lydia is gone forever, I think. But knowing even this much is a great comfort."

"Then what of your lack of breeding?" asked Lady Catherine, drawing Elizabeth's attention back to her.

"If you will pardon me," said Elizabeth, "but I believe that is a matter between myself and Mr. Darcy. If your nephew does not object to my connections, what are they to anyone else?"

"Do you think so little of his family?"

"I think that Mr. Darcy is capable of directing his own affairs, Lady Catherine. You are connected to him, yes, and his other relations obviously have a claim on him as well. But Mr. Darcy is his own man and may choose for himself what he requires in a wife. If I am that choice, why should I not accept with alacrity, knowing the happiness which awaits me as the wife to such a fine man?"

"Does duty mean so little to you? Are you not concerned about making my nephew the scorn of the world?"

"I highly doubt the world cares enough of our doings to censure us, Lady Catherine. There may be some naysayers, but I dare say we will meet them with fortitude and good humor."

Lady Catherine sighed and sank back into her chair. Little though Elizabeth might have credited it, it seemed the lady had no more arrows in her quiver. It was far easier to convince her than Elizabeth might have expected.

"It seems you—neither of you—will be moved. I suppose I have little choice but to accept Darcy's choice or risk a schism in the family."

"It is as I have told you, Lady Catherine," said Mr. Darcy. "I will not be browbeaten into doing what you want. Besides, Anne has little desire herself to be married to anyone, let alone me. She remembers far too well some of the escapades in which we engaged when we were young to see me as a marriage partner. And her health is far too indifferent to allow her to marry."

"Hard though it is to hear of my daughter's inadequacy, I suppose you are not incorrect."

"Do not call her inadequate," replied Mr. Darcy. "Those physical limitations which govern her life are unfortunate. But her wit is keen and her intellect is unaffected by her body's infirmity. She is a wonderful cousin, Aunt. I simply do not wish her for a wife."

"Lady Catherine looked long and hard at Mr. Darcy, and then nodded, albeit slowly. "I suppose you mean to have a Christmas bride?"

"That has not yet been determined," said Mr. Darcy. He looked at Elizabeth, who returned his affection in full measure. "But I believe an announcement will not be too long in coming."

"Then it is well that you have given me something I can mold into a proper wife for you."

"I prefer Miss Bennet the way she is now," said Mr. Darcy, his head whipping back to look at Lady Catherine in alarm.

"Nonsense," was his aunt's firm reply. "While I will acknowledge that Miss Bennet seems a good, intelligent sort of girl, she does not have the experience of moving in society. As such, she requires guidance. I will step forward to ensure the families of Darcy, Fitzwilliam, and de Bourgh are not disgraced."

While Mr. Darcy looked at his aunt with horror, privately Elizabeth was more amused than insulted. The success in persuading his aunt to accept his choice was not an insignificant victory, and if the price was to submit to this woman's "assistance," then so be it. It could have been much worse.

CHAPTER XIV

*L*ady Catherine's assistance was, indeed, ubiquitous. Those final few days before Christmas, Elizabeth discovered just how intent upon dispensing her wisdom Lady Catherine was. While she had not precisely doubted Mr. Darcy's account, it had crossed Elizabeth's mind that he was exaggerating the extent of it. But, if anything, it seems he underestimated the lady's inclination to be of use.

It was fortunate, indeed, that Elizabeth did not spend much time at Mr. Darcy's house, for she thought the amusement she derived from the lady's ridiculousness would wane quickly. Whenever she was within reach of the lady's voice, she found herself the recipient of her instructions and advice, even when further questions on her part revealed that Lady Catherine had no knowledge of the subject herself!

But Elizabeth only visited Darcy house once before Christmas, and as such, she was spared the full measure of Lady Catherine's officiousness. As the day was quickly approaching, there was little time for visits to and fro, and Mr. Darcy seemed quite content to come to her rather than greeting her at his house.

"My cousin, Anne, has also come to town with Lady Catherine," informed Mr. Darcy the day following Lady Catherine's arrival. "It is something of a holiday for her, as she rarely leaves Kent."

"I might have thought your aunt would take a final opportunity to see her dreams realized," teased Elizabeth. "After all, with you both under the same roof together, she might never have a better chance."

"Ah, but you forget that I have visited my aunt's estate every year for several weeks. Had she intended to use such underhanded means, she could have made an attempt during any of those visits."

"Then I suppose you are reprieved!" said Elizabeth. "Perhaps you may enjoy this visit without the threat of her insistence hanging over your heads."

"That is my hope. My relationship with my cousin has suffered over the years due to her mother's unreasoning demands. We were quite close as children, and I hope we will become so again."

During those remaining days before Christmas, Elizabeth was once again struck by the notion that the entire city was somehow gripped by the spirit of the season. While Elizabeth had never resided in London during Christmas and had never witnessed those in the city during the season, she fancied she witnessed others taking the trouble to be a little kinder, with a caring word, or a jauntily spoken "Happy Christmas" on the tip of the tongue. As she went about her own life, she gave as much of the cheer of the season to others as she could spare.

Even when she and Mr. Darcy walked in the nearby park, everyone with whom they met nodded, or doffed their hat with a hearty wish for joy during the season. They were even passed by a young man who walked quickly and with a seriousness of purpose, though when they came upon him a moment later, meeting a lady by the bench, it was clear that she was not nearly as happy with him. Elizabeth and her beau hurried past them, eager to avoid interrupting a conversation which appeared like it would be fraught with heightened emotions.

"It seems not everyone is happy this season, Mr. Darcy," said Elizabeth. "I am afraid my faith is shattered, for it has seemed to me of late that everyone is filled with the spirit."

"And yet, the world we live in is not always a happy one," replied Mr. Darcy.

"Should the spirit of the season fill all men *all* the year round, I dare say they would be happier."

"You are correct, of course. In the future, whenever life is pressing down on us, I suggest we remember your words and try to recapture the spirit of goodwill to all."

Elizabeth blushed at his reference to their future lives and their presence in each other's. To keep her countenance, she turned the topic, and they continued to speak, to take each other's measure and learn more of the other. Interspersed with their conversations were more intimate moments. Mr. Darcy kissed her again several times when they could be assured of being alone. Eager as she was for his affections, Elizabeth participated in these moments eagerly, though she knew they were technically forbidden. They were not even courting yet!

And yet the fact that he had not yet asked for a courtship at the very least was a source of some curiosity for Elizabeth. A few weeks earlier she might have been concerned, wondering if he was having second thoughts. He had not hidden his admiration, nor had he stinted in showering his affection on her. Elizabeth did not know why he was yet reticent to take the next step, but she determined to enjoy his determined courting and allow him to come to the point in his own time.

Christmas Eve finally arrived, and Elizabeth found herself as excited as she had been since she was a child, anticipating the wonder of Christmas. During the day, she and her aunt spent their day with the children, engaged in creating some simple crafts for the children and eating Christmas treats which they would not be allowed on a normal day. Her uncle spent the morning in his offices finishing a final few tasks before Christmas, and he joined them after luncheon.

For dinner, Mr. Darcy joined them, entering to the pleased greetings of all, though Elizabeth noted his eyes rarely left her. They dined together, the children joining them in making a merry party, after which they were to go to the church for the Christmas Eve services.

"I hope Georgiana is well?" asked Elizabeth as they sat down to their dinner. "I expected her to join you tonight."

"Georgiana had other plans for this evening," said Mr. Darcy. "I am certain her own evening will be as merry as ours, Miss Bennet, and she shall join us tomorrow."

Though she was confused, Elizabeth nodded, accepting his explanation, assuming Lady Catherine had mandated Georgiana's presence with her that evening. Indeed, she could think of no other explanation, for she knew Georgiana was not out and would not attend other parties by herself, though she supposed her companion could accompany her.

Once dinner was completed, the company made their way from the house and down the street to the church which had previously been

Elizabeth's refuge. The denizens of the neighborhood had turned out in force in all their finery, many of whom were known to her aunt and uncle. Greetings were exchanged, and Mr. Darcy introduced to many new acquaintances. Elizabeth noted that while he was a reticent man in general, he was perfectly amiable and pleasant, even considering these people were far below him in society. A few of them might even have recognized his name, from their reaction to the introductions.

They sat down to the service and listened to the parson's sermon, the voices of the choir rising up through the rafters and washing them all with the love of the savior. At the appropriate times, they consulted their prayer books and sang the beloved Christmas carols, raising their voices in praise. Once again, Mr. Darcy sang with a rich baritone which, while it was not trained, was perfectly pleasant.

After the service, they stayed at the church for some few moments, speaking to those who were known to the Gardiners. While Mr. Darcy was an unknown quantity, it seemed he was easily discernable as a man of some consequence, provoking many more who sought his acquaintance, even those who were not well known to Mr. and Mrs. Gardiner. But Mr. Darcy bore all their curiosity and spoke to all and sundry with perfect composure. The most curious of the supplicants was the pastor, Mr. Forbes, who approached as they were about to leave.

"Happy Christmas, Mr. Gardiner, Mrs. Gardiner," said he. Then he turned to Elizabeth. "Miss Bennet, Happy Christmas. Will you not introduce me to your friend?"

Elizabeth performed the office, and the two men bowed to each other. For some few moments, they did not speak. But the substance of their interested looks contained a quality Elizabeth could not quite understand. There was interest, she thought, but as she watched, she had the impression of two predators circling warily around each other.

"I hope that whatever problem led you to the church the other day has been resolved?" said Mr. Forbes at length, turning to Elizabeth.

Surprised he would bring it up, Elizabeth nodded and said: "Yes, it has."

"I saw you in the attitude of prayer just before Mr. Darcy arrived," said Mr. Forbes, his eyes darting another look in Mr. Darcy's direction. "Had Mr. Darcy not come, I would have approached you to determine whether you needed assistance."

"As you can see, I am well," replied Elizabeth.

Mr. Forbes again paused, his eyes searching Elizabeth's. "I hope you do not consider it an impertinence, Miss Bennet, but I wish to ensure your wellbeing. You have not been . . . unduly put upon?"

"No," said Elizabeth at the same time Mr. Darcy frowned.

While he recognized Mr. Darcy's displeasure, Mr. Forbes did not back down. "I do not mean to accuse, Mr. Darcy. But while Miss Bennet seemed cheered after you came, I was witness to certain . . . improprieties within the boundaries of a house of God. The question is not unreasonable."

"Mr. Darcy was not the cause of my distress, Mr. Forbes," said Elizabeth quickly. Then she looked to Mr. Darcy and smiled, which he returned with a certain wryness. "At least, Mr. Darcy did not provoke my distress due to any reason you suspect. Regardless, the matter has been resolved."

"Very well, then," said Mr. Forbes. He peered into Elizabeth's eyes again for a moment before he bowed to her. "Then it seems I am to wish you every happiness, Miss Bennet. I hope you do not blame me for inquiring as to your peace of mind."

"Not at all," said Elizabeth. She noted that Mr. Darcy did not say anything, but the look he was giving the parson was not unfriendly, so she allowed the matter to drop.

With those final words, Mr. Forbes excused himself, and Mr. Darcy escorted Elizabeth outside with the Gardiners following. They reached the street and began walking, and while she stepped at Mr. Darcy's side, Elizabeth's mind continued to revert to the strange scene which had just played out in the church. She could not quite make out what happened. Mr. Darcy, however, soon made his interpretation known.

"Had I known I must fight for your hand, Miss Bennet, I would have armed myself accordingly."

Shocked, Elizabeth looked up at the gentleman and blurted: "Mr. Forbes? I have no notion of what you speak, sir?"

The raised eyebrow Mr. Darcy directed at Elizabeth spoke to his disbelief. "Have you had no indication of Mr. Forbes's admiration?"

"None whatsoever!" exclaimed Elizabeth. "Truly, it appears you see things which do not exist, sir."

"I beg to differ, Miss Bennet. It is clear to me that Mr. Forbes had some interest in you at the very least."

"But I have not spoken to him often, and he has never made any interest known to *me*."

"And yet it exists." Elizabeth made to protest again, but Mr. Darcy said: "I am a man, Miss Bennet—one who is in love with a woman. Allow me the discernment to understand when another man admires a woman, especially when he admires a woman that *I* admire!"

There was nothing Elizabeth could say to that, especially when her laughing uncle interjected from where he walked behind them with Mrs. Gardiner: "Mr. Darcy has the right of it, Lizzy. Forbes has spoken to me of you, and while he was never overt, it was clear to me that his inquiries were not of the casual kind."

Mr. Gardiner laughed. "It is to his general reticence I attribute his failure to speak to you of it—that and his careful nature."

"Why did you not tell me?"

"Because he did not speak openly," replied Mr. Gardiner with a shrug. "I believe there was some interest in securing himself financially before he would consider taking a wife. He is, as you know, new to the parish."

"We had some hope," added Elizabeth's aunt, "that in the future he might be persuaded to act."

"I never knew any of it," said Elizabeth, feeling a little bewildered.

"Nor did we wish to raise your hopes." Then Mrs. Gardiner smiled at Mr. Darcy. "Then again, everything seems to have worked out for the best. Perhaps you would have been content with Mr. Forbes, had he made any overtures. However, I cannot imagine it could have been what I see before my eyes at present."

"Quite so, Mrs. Gardiner," said Mr. Darcy. "Miss Bennet's happiness will always be my first priority."

"By my account, sir," said Elizabeth archly, "there is not anything formal between us."

Much to Elizabeth's annoyance, Mr. Darcy did not immediately respond. Instead, he smiled at her and continued to walk, maintaining his silence. Soon they arrived at the door to the Gardiner townhouse, and while it was late, her aunt and uncle allowed them a few moments to say their farewells. They climbed the steps and entered the house, leaving Elizabeth and Mr. Darcy alone on the street.

"Until tomorrow, Miss Bennet," said Mr. Darcy. "After our time with the children and Father Christmas," he winked at her, "we shall retire to my house for the rest of the day. I am anticipating it keenly."

"As am I, Mr. Darcy."

Mr. Darcy bowed over her hand, bestowing a lingering kiss on its back. When he rose, he showed her a loving smile and squeezed her hand. Then he leaned in and spoke softly, though ensuring he was heard.

"Tomorrow will be a most auspicious day, Miss Bennet. I find I can hardly wait."

Then he released her hand, turned and boarded his coach, but not before giving her a long look. Then the carriage was off, clattering down the street, bearing her heart away. Elizabeth climbed the stairs slowly, her eyes remaining fixed upon the conveyance dwindling in the distance. It was some time after it rolled out of sight before she entered the house.

The children were excited to see them the next morning. Once again, Mrs. Gardiner and Georgiana had accompanied Elizabeth and Mr. Darcy to the Foundling Hospital, finding the children waiting for them in the main hall. There were several other young ladies and a gentleman or two in attendance that day — though thankfully not Lady Frances or Miss Howard — and it was clear to Elizabeth's eyes that her party was the one they were most excited to see.

"Miss Bennet!" squealed Genevieve, throwing herself into Elizabeth's arms when she stepped into the room, the other girls crowding behind. "Happy Christmas! How happy we all are to see you!"

Mrs. Mason, the matron, appeared about to reprimand the girl when Elizabeth smiled at her to inform her she was not displeased. Mrs. Mason nodded, and while she did look pointedly at Genevieve, she did not comment on the matter. Divesting herself of the young girl, Elizabeth smiled at her, and at the other children, greeting them with a little more understated enthusiasm than Genevieve had shown.

"Hello, Children, and Happy Christmas. I hope you are all ready to celebrate the season today."

A chorus in the affirmative met Elizabeth's declaration, and the children were guided back to the hall where several games had been set up in anticipation of the day's festivities. There was a hearty dinner, for which Elizabeth knew Mr. Darcy had pledged himself, an action which earned the gentleman her heartfelt thanks. Then in various locations, games had been set up for the children's entertainment.

In all, it was a joyous celebration, and likely more than the children had seen in previous years stay at the Foundling Hospital. There was laughter aplenty at their antics, and the adults even partook in a game of snap-dragon to the oohs and ahs of the watching children. The lights were dimmed, and when the brandy was set ablaze, the blue flames fascinated those watching. While Elizabeth did not capture the most treats — that distinction was reserved for Georgiana — she thought she acquitted herself well.

Later that morning, Mr. Darcy slipped from the room, and when he returned, he was dressed in the costume of Father Christmas. The children squealed and laughed when he entered, producing the surprises they had purchased the previous week. In the end, each of the children was satisfied, for the girls had new dolls, while the boys were presented with stick horses.

It was about noon when Elizabeth's party finally said farewell to the children and made their way to Mr. Darcy's carriage to return to Gracechurch Street, and from thence to Mr. Darcy house. When the carriage lurched into motion, Elizabeth turned a smile on Mr. Darcy.

"I had no idea you were so versatile, Mr. Darcy. Had I not known otherwise, I could have sworn you were actually Father Christmas!"

Mr. Darcy waggled his eyebrows and said: "Merely one of my many talents, Miss Bennet. I hope to be in a position to show you more of what I am capable."

They all laughed at his words. "If you would stop delaying, I am certain Elizabeth would have a lifetime to learn of your capabilities."

Though Elizabeth turned a mock glare on Georgiana, Mr. Darcy only smiled and lounged back on his seat. "All in good time, Georgiana dearest. Before I take such a step, I must ensure that Miss Bennet and I are compatible. You did put out mistletoe this year, did you not?"

The three tormentors all laughed at Elizabeth's embarrassment, and her glares seemed to do nothing to quell their mirth. "Of course, I did!" said Georgiana.

Mrs. Gardiner, however, winked and said: "By all accounts, you should already be quite familiar with such things, Mr. Darcy. I do hope, however, you receive ample opportunity to test your *compatibility* today."

"I am not certain I wish to encourage poor behavior, Mr. Darcy," said Elizabeth with a superior sniff, one very much like Miss Bingley's.

"Remember, Miss Bennet," said Mr. Darcy, "you cannot refuse a kiss if you are caught under the mistletoe."

"No, but I can avoid the infernal plant altogether."

Mr. Darcy appeared very much like a boy who had had his favorite toy stolen at Elizabeth's declaration. This, of course, prompted more laughter, to which Elizabeth was happy to join in.

"You shall just have to catch me, Mr. Darcy," said Elizabeth.

The look which he bestowed upon her suggested he would be diligent in tracking her movements that afternoon. As the only single man in the celebration, with herself as the only single woman, she anticipated the game of cat and mouse keenly. And Elizabeth planned to be captured at least once or twice, though she would not tell *him* that, of course.

The governess had the children prepared when they arrived at the Gardiners' house, and they were soon able to depart. Elizabeth continued to ride in the Darcy carriage with Mr. and Miss Darcy, along with Abigail, who insisted on traveling with them. This set off a round of protests among the other children, who insisted *they* be allowed to go to. In the end, it was decided that the girls would both ride in the Darcy carriage, while the two boys rode with their parents.

The journey across the city was accomplished quickly, and soon they were all disembarking in front of Mr. Darcy's house. The children were bustled into the house quickly to remove them from the elements, and they doffed their winter wear, handing it to the waiting servants. It was there, Elizabeth began to notice something strange in the behavior of both Mr. Darcy and his sister. They both watched her closely as if assuring themselves of her presence. For that matter, the Gardiners were no less attentive. It seemed like they were all expectation, but of what Elizabeth could not determine.

"Why do you all watch me in such a fashion?" demanded Elizabeth, fixing them all with a suspicious glare.

"Because, Miss Bennet," said Mr. Darcy, taking the lead, "we are all eager to witness your reaction to what we have to show you."

"And what is that?"

Mr. Darcy smiled, a tender expression which made Elizabeth's knees feel weak. "We, all of us, have conspired together to present you with a gift for Christmas, a gift we are certain will be priceless, given your recent past."

Surprised and suddenly emotional at the revelation, Elizabeth blinked away tears. "I have no notion of what you have all done, but the sentiment has quite undone me!"

"You should pull yourself together, Lizzy, dearest," said Mrs. Gardiner. She stepped forward and embraced Elizabeth, her uncle close behind, smiling broadly. "If you are emotional now at the merest mention of a gift, I cannot imagine what your reaction will be when confronted by the reality of it."

"That is all very well!" exclaimed Elizabeth. "But I still do not know what it is!"

"Oh, no," said he with a wink. "We will not spoil the surprise, for we have all anticipated this day. Your surprise is waiting in the sitting-room. Shall we not go there now?"

Not trusting herself to speak, Elizabeth nodded, allowing Mr. Darcy to lead her away toward the sitting room. Elizabeth found herself alive with anticipation, though she did not know why. Their words suggested it was more than some trinket or physical gift, but she could not imagine what it was. For a moment, she even pictured a moment when they had entered the room together, only to have Mr. Darcy sink to one knee and propose. What a gift that would be!

"It is right in here, Miss Bennet," said Mr. Darcy as they approached the room.

The footman stationed at the door opened it and fixed a wide smile on Elizabeth as she passed through the door. She was distracted for a moment, wondering what the man could possibly know about what was waiting there for her. As such, it took several moments for Elizabeth to realize more people were waiting in the room than she had expected.

Then a much-beloved voice reached her ears, one she had not heard in far too long.

"Lizzy!"

CHAPTER XV

*A*bewildered Elizabeth had no time to respond before she was engulfed in an embrace. While she could not normally be termed as a person who needed much explanation to understand, it was a few moments before she could determine who had caught her up so fiercely.

"Jane?" asked Elizabeth in a tremulous voice.

"Oh, Lizzy! How I have missed you!"

The sound of laughter reached Elizabeth's ears, and she realized at that moment that not only had she been seized by her elder sister, but others had approached as well. When Elizabeth opened her eyes, to her great bafflement, she saw her two remaining sisters with her mother crowding around them. Cries of greeting rose, and the tears of the five women mingled together as they were reunited after many months of being sundered. And in the background stood Mr. Bingley, his joyous countenance watching the gathering with his usual exuberance. Mr. Darcy and his sister, along with Lady Catherine and another lady with whom Elizabeth had not yet made an acquaintance, also watched, and Elizabeth saw with a kind of detached amusement that even Lady Catherine did not appear unmoved by what was happening.

"Lizzy!" came the excited voice of her mother, though it was understated, unlike the shrieks Mrs. Bennet often released. "Finally you are here! What a lovely house and a wonderful man you have caught for yourself!"

Elizabeth could not help but laugh at her mother—though she could easily see Lady Catherine was not amused—and she partially disengaged from her sister to pull her mother close. For the first time, Elizabeth could ever remember, Mrs. Bennet allowed herself to be drawn close, tears streaming down her face unabashedly. Then Mary and Kitty were also embraced as the five Bennet ladies gathered in as tightly as they could possibly manage.

"But I do not understand," managed Elizabeth at length. "How could you all be here, of all places?" Turning to her beloved sister, Elizabeth smiled, though she felt as if she would burst into tears at any moment. "When did you come from the north?"

"It was all Mr. Darcy's doing!" exclaimed Mrs. Bennet, turning a warm look on the man who, Elizabeth was certain, she hoped would soon be her son-in-law. "I declare I have never been so surprised as when I received a letter from my brother and Mr. Darcy, inviting us here. What a wonderful man you have found, Lizzy!"

"Well, then," said Lady Catherine, seemingly at the end of her patience with the display of the Bennet ladies, "perhaps we should all sit together for the explanations."

It was a surprise, but Mrs. Bennet instantly quieted at the lady's words. They all repaired to the assortment of sofas and chairs situated near a roaring fireplace and settled themselves in. Jane and Elizabeth, after so many months of separation, could not bear to be parted, and Kitty and Mary held themselves close to their elder sisters. But before they could begin any conversation concerning the day's events, Mr. Bingley stepped forward and kneeled in front of Elizabeth.

"Lizzy, I wish to apologize to you, as I already have your mother and sisters, for my terrible decision to separate you all last spring."

"Oh, Mr. Bingley," cried Elizabeth, her heart going out to the earnest man kneeling before her. "I do not blame you. Anyone would have made the same decision under such circumstances."

"Perhaps they would have," agreed the genial man. "But I like to think I hold myself to a higher standard."

"Should absolution be required," said Elizabeth warmly, "I offer it wholeheartedly."

Mr. Bingley grinned and patted her hands. "Being witness to the meeting between you and your sisters, I realize that I should never have insisted on it in the first place." He paused and smiled at Jane. "My dear wife never protested my decision, but it was not long before I realized she was made deeply unhappy by it."

"I missed my family," was Jane's quiet interjection.

"And I am heartily sorry that I ever insisted you abandon them. That shall not happen again, I assure you. Especially since it seems we shall soon have a happy announcement involving my dearest friend."

The look Mr. Bingley fixed on Mr. Darcy was teasing, but Mr. Darcy only nodded in what could be deemed a complacent manner. Seeing this, Mr. Bingley shook his head. "You were much more amusing when you took offense to such teasing."

The company laughed, though Lady Catherine's huff could be heard above the gaiety. For his part, Mr. Darcy's responding smile was positively smug. Mr. Bingley shook his head again in mock annoyance and turned back to Elizabeth.

"Now we are all reunited, and we shall never be separated again." A dark look came over his face. "Though certain members will not be allowed into our presence again."

Confused, Elizabeth looked at him wondering to whom he was referring. Mr. Bingley understood her question for he quickly responded: "I discovered some months ago that my sister had been behaving in a very unkind manner toward my dearest wife."

"We do not need to discuss this, Charles," said Jane, ever the peacemaker.

"But we do," was her husband's firm reply. "It was all small matters, of course, but Caroline had been interfering in Jane's ability to manage the house, saying unkind things to her about your family, trying to turn *me* against my wife." Mr. Bingley snorted with disdain, an incongruous action in one so easy of temper as he. "When I discovered it, I banished her from my home, never to return. She is with the Hursts now in London, and she had best find herself a husband, for I have washed my hands of her."

"A woman too full of herself is your sister," said Lady Catherine, shaking her head in exasperation. "Never before have I met her like."

"We met her and the Hursts on Bond Street," said Elizabeth quietly. In her heart, she was offended all over by Miss Bingley. But there was no use in speaking to an obviously penitent Mr. Bingley of the matter.

"I did not realize that," said Mr. Bingley, turning to look at Mr. Darcy.

Mr. Darcy only shrugged. "The subject never arose, my friend."

"Let us not speak of this, Charles," said Jane. "Sometime in the future, you might find it in your heart to forgive your sister. At present, it is a happy occasion, and I would like to speak of happy subjects."

Finally, Mr. Bingley was of a mind to relinquish the floor, and he nodded in fond agreement at his wife. "You are too good, Jane, but it shall be as you say. Allow me to say how happy I am to be back with you all. I have missed you exceedingly!"

Mr. Bingley rose and moved away, allowing the sisters to remain together. Elizabeth looked about at all the dear faces, and the confusion she had felt upon entering once again welled up within her.

"I cannot express my happiness at seeing you all here. But I am unable to account for it, and if you all do not explain it to me at once, I fear I shall burst from curiosity!"

Again the room was filled with the laughter of the company, for most of these people knew her intimately, and were well aware of her character and her dislike for ignorance. The only two who were not well acquainted with her were Lady Catherine and the woman Elizabeth presumed was her daughter. For Lady Catherine's part, she watched them all with something akin to resigned revulsion, but for the younger woman's part, she watched Elizabeth with evident interest.

"As I told you before, Lizzy," said Mrs. Bennet in a far calmer voice than Elizabeth might have expected, "it was all Mr. Darcy's doing. He, with my brother's assistance, invited us to town, offered his house as our lodgings while we are here, and sent a carriage to Essex for our comfort."

"We knew how much you missed your family," said Georgiana. "So we did our best to ensure you could be with them again for Christmas. It is our gift you to."

Elizabeth felt herself choking up, though she managed a smile at Georgiana. "And I thank you for it, dearest Georgiana. No other gift could be so precious."

Then Elizabeth turned to her aunt and fixed her with a pointed gaze. "Then why did you suggest my mother and sisters visit in the new year since you were obviously aware of this?"

"At the time, the scheme had not yet been made known to me, Lizzy. But I gave it my firm support when I was made aware."

"For our part," said Mr. Bingley, "you can imagine my surprise when I received a letter from my close friend, requesting our presence for Christmas." Mr. Bingley paused, as if suppressing laughter, and proceeded to say: "You will not be surprised, Sister, when I inform you that I considered the matter for all of twenty seconds before dashing off a reply via express."

"And a most perplexing missive it was!" said Mr. Darcy with a laugh. "I always thought I was proficient at deciphering your handwriting, but that letter proved how wrong I was. All I was able to determine was that you agreed, though, for all I could tell, you would not arrive until the turn of the century!"

The merriment of the company was released again at Mr. Darcy's jest, Mr. Bingley laughing the loudest. The explanations having been completed. The Bennet sisters, excited at being gathered together again were eager to hear the news of the others, while all around them conversations sprang up, or those with whom they were gathered listened with indulgent smiles, interjecting comments here and there. The biggest news was offered by Jane herself when she informed them she was with child.

"You may all expect to be aunts by about April."

"That is wonderful news, Jane!" exclaimed Elizabeth, echoed by her sisters. Elizabeth drew away a little, inspecting her sister for signs of what she was being told.

It seemed Jane understood the reason for her scrutiny, for she gave Elizabeth a gentle smile. "The midwife informed me it is not unusual for a woman to retain her figure until well into her first confinement. Though I am not anticipating the feeling of being as big as a house, I will bear it for my dear Charles and our mutual desire for a family."

Laughing at Jane's sally, Charles was quick to say: "You will never be any less beautiful in my eyes, even should you grow as large as *two* houses!"

"I am very happy for you, dearest Sister. I know you shall be an excellent mother."

Of Kitty and Mary, there was little to say. The sisters had lived quietly in Hertfordshire with their mother, and as their circumstances were much reduced from what they had been before, there had not been much society for them. Kitty was eager to show Elizabeth the portfolio she had accumulated since their sundering, to which Elizabeth promised she would be happy to view it. As for Mary, their family's troubles seemed to have curbed Mary's moralizing and need to insert little homilies into the conversation. She would ever be a serious-minded young woman, but some of those quirks which had irritated Elizabeth in the past had been tempered. When she learned that Georgiana was a musician, Mary's conversation turned to the younger girl, and they discussed playing together. Elizabeth hoped that she would be able to provide the benefit of masters to assist Mary in improving.

Mrs. Bennet was the one whom Elizabeth recognized the least. During the initial greetings, she was largely silent, watching her daughters happily, but inserting little to the conversation. As the company relaxed and began to separate into their various groups, her mother approached her, favoring her with a lopsided smile, as if fighting back emotion.

"How happy I am to see you again, Lizzy," said her mother, grasping her hands and clasping them tightly. "I have found I shall forever miss your father, though at times he vexed me greatly. But having my two oldest and most beautiful girls living at such a distance has taught me that I do not wish to be parted again."

"I can well understand your sentiments, Mama," said Elizabeth. "Our reunion with Jane means we are now a family again, never to be sundered."

"I hope so, Lizzy." Then Mrs. Bennet proved she had not changed in essentials, for she exclaimed: "And this house is so wonderful and charming."

She leaned in close, saying in a low voice: "I dare say Lady Lucas would be positively green with envy should she see this house of which my daughter will one day be mistress. In the end, I have no doubt I have triumphed!"

Then Mrs. Bennet gave Elizabeth an embrace and walked away, joining Lady Catherine where she sat on a nearby sofa. It was clear from the lady's pinched look she had not appreciated Mrs. Bennet's words, but from what Elizabeth could see, she did not castigate her either. Instead, Lady Catherine spoke, and Mrs. Bennet listened, and while she did not know what she thought of Lady Catherine teaching her mother proper behavior, she decided it was not a matter that should be investigated too closely.

It was also Elizabeth's pleasure to meet Miss Anne de Bourgh for the first time, and while she had heard much from the Darcy siblings concerning their cousin, she was interested in forming her own opinion of the young woman. That initial opinion was nothing but positive, considering the woman's words.

"I feel I must thank you, Miss Bennet," said she. "For you have freed me from my mother's constant efforts to wed me to my cousin."

The huff Elizabeth heard from behind Miss de Bourgh indicated that Lady Catherine was not unaware of her daughter's words. The other woman only smiled, however, and ignored her mother.

"Nothing is decided yet," was Elizabeth's cautious reply.

"No, but it soon will be. I hope we will become friends and that you will come and visit my mother and me in Kent." Miss de Bourgh gave her a sad smile.

"We would be happy to," assured Elizabeth, pressing her hands against Miss de Bourgh's.

In due time, the party was called into the dining room for a sumptuous Christmas feast. Mr. Darcy, eschewing precedence, escorted not only Mrs. Bennet, but also Elizabeth to the dining room, seating them on either side of himself. At the other end of the table, Georgiana took her place as the house's mistress, though her mischievous grin at Elizabeth suggested she thought she would not occupy that chair for much longer.

The dinner was a triumph, as the cook had provided them with all the traditional dishes for their Christmas feast, with a large plum pudding to finish their dinner. Elizabeth was not the only one who groaned at the end of the meal, having eaten her fill of the excellent fare.

The usual games were dispensed with that evening by common consent, for they were all too interested in renewing the bonds strained by distance or making new acquaintances. As the only gentlemen in attendance, Mr. Darcy could often be found with Mr. Bingley and Mr. Gardiner, but Elizabeth was heartened to see that he was taking pains to come to know those members of her family with whom he was not already familiar. Even Mrs. Bennet received his attention, though Elizabeth wondered what he would think when her usual exuberance returned. For the present, however, it seemed like an accord had been reached, one no doubt encouraged by their mutual love for Elizabeth herself.

At length, Elizabeth also remembered the gifts she had so painstakingly chosen for the Darcys, and she presented them with all the fanfare due the occasion. "I am sure these are not the equal of the gift you have given to me, but I hope you will have some small use of them."

Georgiana's present consisted of a novel she had seen her future sister admiring at the bookstore, along with a selection of sheet music for the pianoforte she knew the younger girl would enjoy. With a happy laugh, Georgiana accepted them and sat down with Mary, both poring over the music, excitedly speaking of how they would learn them as soon as possible.

As for Mr. Darcy, the gift Elizabeth had agonized over choosing consisted of several handkerchiefs and a watch fob. But she had taken the impersonal gift and embroidered Mr. Darcy's initials with those she would soon bear herself in one corner. Mr. Darcy fingered the lettering after opening his gift, seemingly at a loss for words.

"I hope I am not presumptuous in the content of my gifts, Mr. Darcy," said she with an impish smile.

"Not presumptuous at all, Miss Bennet." He paused and grinned. "I will treasure them always, though I hope you will forgive me if I do not use them until a certain event has taken place."

"Not at all!" exclaimed Elizabeth with a laugh. "In fact, you may wish to simply have them framed as a reminder of my impertinence."

"I hardly think I will require a reminder," was his dry reply. "Now, as we are speaking of gifts, I have something of which I wish to make you aware." Elizabeth's questioning look was enough to prompt him to continue: "I have received a letter from my steward at Pemberley, whom I asked to look into certain situations for children at the hospital. There are several, which we may see the children installed in early in the New Year, and one in particular which I believe might suit your dearest little Genevieve. I hope this — "

Mr. Darcy's words were interrupted by a loud grunt when Elizabeth threw herself at him, laughing and crying at the same time. "Can it be true?" asked she as she attempted to wipe the tears from her eyes.

"Yes, it is." Mr. Darcy bestowed on her a tender smile. "My steward and his wife recently suffered the loss of a child, and have agreed to meet Genevieve with the intent of taking her into their home. Should you be agreeable, she will live in their cottage as their daughter, and when the time comes, she will have every advantage she may derive from our patronage."

"I do wish it, Mr. Darcy," said Elizabeth, her happiness near to overwhelming her. "I hope we are in a position to continue to help those unfortunate children."

"As you suggested, the process should be formalized. We will not end our affiliation with the hospital, so I am certain we can determine the means by which those children have all the opportunity in life they wish to have."

It was all and more Elizabeth had ever wished, and she expressed herself to her suitor as any woman violently in love could be expected to do. Her heart was full — Elizabeth found she could not ask for more.

Later in the evening, Elizabeth, who found herself speaking with her younger sisters and Georgiana, animatedly, was ushered to a certain place in the room. Though she protested this was not how it was done, her objections fell on deaf ears.

"No, Lizzy," said Georgiana amid a peal of laughter. "William is the only single man in attendance tonight, and as he has no interest in any single lady other than you, it is up to you to utilize the mistletoe. You would not wish the effort to go to waste, would you?"

"Georgiana!" exclaimed Elizabeth, wondering what Lady Catherine would say about such a display.

"Of course, she would not," said Mr. Darcy.

As one, Elizabeth and Georgiana turned to see Mr. Darcy watching them, a grin fixed on them both. To Elizabeth, it seemed like the man was supremely confident, the perfect of male self-assurance. While she might have perversely thought to put him in his place, Elizabeth was too mesmerized by the sight of his loving look at her to do any such thing.

"And you are correct," continued Mr. Darcy in a conversational tone. "I have no interest in the other single ladies in attendance tonight, though I do sympathize with them." He turned a grin on Georgiana and added: "In your case, however, I am quite happy you will not expect to be married this year, for I have no intention of giving up your company just yet."

Georgiana only smirked at him and nodded toward Elizabeth before turning away in a twirl of girlish skirts. Had Elizabeth looked about, she would have noted the attention of the entire company on her and Mr. Darcy, most with barely restrained glee. Lady Catherine might have been, as usual, more than a little sour at what she was seeing, but Elizabeth was certain the lady was becoming accustomed to the death of her dreams.

However, Elizabeth was able to see nothing but Mr. Darcy, his presence driving out any thoughts of the others in the room. He stepped forward, his eyes never leaving hers, and stopped in front of her, looking down with tenderness and love. In one smooth motion, Mr. Darcy reached up and pulled several berries from the plant above, displaying them in one hand for her to see.

"Shall we count the berries, Miss Bennet? Or shall we simply agree that all your kisses belong to me?"

"That is hardly the establish mode, Mr. Darcy," teased Elizabeth. "I do not know if I should agree to a kiss when the rules have been blatantly disregarded."

"Miss Elizabeth?"

"Yes?"

"Sometimes you talk too much."

Then Mr. Darcy leaned down and kissed her on the lips, prompting the cheering of the rest of the party. It was no chaste peck either, for though his display did not breach propriety, he lingered, his lips pressed against hers as Elizabeth sighed and melted into his embrace. For a moment, the others in the room and the very world about them seemed to cease to exist. Then he pulled away from her, his hand reaching up to caress her cheek as he gazed into her eyes.

"Do you mean to forever silence me in such a manner, Mr. Darcy?" asked Elizabeth.

"If I must," replied Mr. Darcy.

Elizabeth gave a great show of considering the matter before she said: "It *is* effective, I must own, though hardly conventional. And while it is permissible under a sprig of mistletoe, I rather think we shall scandalize the world if you do so in a public venue."

"Then I shall simply be required to ensure there is always mistletoe overhead. How many sprigs do you think I may procure to ensure every place you might stand will be covered?"

A laugh bubbled up from Elizabeth's breast. "While you may do that in your own home, silly though it sounds, surely you cannot make mistletoe appear wherever I might go."

"Then I suppose we shall simply need to scandalize society." Mr. Darcy grinned. "They could do with a little excitement anyway."

"Just say the word, Mr. Darcy. I am likely to be despised as an outsider regardless. So if your provincial wife scandalizes society, they will simply blame it on my origins."

Mr. Darcy chuckled and shook his head. "It seems, Miss Bennet, that while we have spoken of putting the horse before the cart before, in this instance that is truly what we are doing now."

"And how do you mean to rectify that deficiency, Mr. Darcy?"

It was a blatant challenge, and Mr. Darcy's grin told Elizabeth that he accepted it without reservation. He proved his willingness without hesitation.

"Then I would ask for your hand in marriage, Miss Bennet. Since you are so thoroughly compromised, I know you must have no other choice than to accept."

Elizabeth laughed and shot him a severe look. "Being kissed under the mistletoe by no means compromises a young woman."

"Are you rejecting me, Miss Bennet?"

"I may receive a better offer," said Elizabeth flippantly.

"Oh, for heaven's sake!" exclaimed Mrs. Bennet. "How can you say such things, Lizzy?"

"Do not concern yourself, Mrs. Bennet," replied Mr. Darcy before Elizabeth could speak. "I know it is incumbent upon me to please a woman worthy of being pleased, and I have every intention of doing so."

Mrs. Bennet's muttering reached Elizabeth's ears, and she could well understand her mother's words, which centered on Elizabeth's perverseness and the fact that she most definitely resembled her father's side of the family. As it was, Elizabeth took that as a compliment and was not displeased at all.

"Miss Elizabeth," began Mr. Darcy, turning his attention back to Elizabeth, "I find myself desperately in love with you and quite wild to be able to call you mine. Will you not end my misery by consenting to my proposal?"

"Why, of course, I will, Mr. Darcy," said Elizabeth. "Now, I notice you have several more berries in your hand. Might I suggest you use them?"

Mr. Darcy did, much to the delight of the company. But Elizabeth had no ability to think of *them*, for she was too caught up in the sensations of Mr. Darcy's love. As she sighed under the ministrations of this man, whose love she prized above all others, Elizabeth thought she felt the gaze of her father upon her, his approval never in doubt. And in the company of her beloved family and the man whom she had found against all odds, Elizabeth was content. The love of this good man and the return of her family were the best gifts of all.

The End

FOR READERS WHO LIKED
A GIFT FOR ELIZABETH

A Tale of Two Courtships
Two sisters, both in danger of losing their hearts. One experiences a courtship which ends quickly in an engagement, the other must struggle against the machinations of others. And one who will do anything to ensure her beloved sister achieves her heart's desire.

Out of Obscurity
Amid the miraculous events of a lost soul returning home, dark forces conspire against a young woman, for her loss was not an accident. A man is moved to action by a boon long denied, determined to avoid being cheated by Miss Elizabeth Bennet again.

Murder at Netherfield
After the ball at Netherfield, a fault in their carriage results in the Bennet family being forced to stay at the Bingley estate, and when a blizzard blows in overnight, the Bennets find themselves stranded there. When a body is found, leading to a string of murders which threaten the lives of those present, Elizabeth and Darcy form an alliance to discover the identity of the murderer and save those they care about most. But the depraved actions of a killer, striking from the shadows, threatens their newly found admiration for each other.

Netherfield's Secret
Elizabeth soon determines that her brother's friend, Fitzwilliam Darcy, suffers from an excess of pride, and it comes as a shock when the man reveals himself to be in love with her. But even that revelation is not as surprising as the secret Netherfield has borne witness to. Netherfield's secret shatters Elizabeth's perception of herself and the world around her, and Mr. Darcy is the only one capable of picking up the pieces.

What Comes Between Cousins
A rivalry springs up between Mr. Darcy and Colonel Fitzwilliam, each determined to win the fair Elizabeth Bennet. As the situation between cousins deteriorates, clarity begins to come for Elizabeth, and she sees Mr. Darcy as the man who will fill all her desires in a husband. But the rivalry between cousins is not the only trouble brewing for Elizabeth.

Whispers of the Heart
A different Bingley party arrives in Hertfordshire leading to a new suitor emerging for the worthiest of the Bennet sisters. As her sister has obtained her happiness, Elizabeth Bennet finds herself thrown into society far above any she might have otherwise expected, which leads her to a new understanding of the enigmatic Mr. Darcy.

For more details, visit
http://www.onegoodsonnet.com/genres/pride-and-prejudice-variations

ALSO BY ONE GOOD SONNET PUBLISHING

THE SMOTHERED ROSE TRILOGY

BOOK 1: THORNY

In this retelling of "Beauty and the Beast," a spoiled boy who is forced to watch over a flock of sheep finds himself more interested in catching the eye of a girl with lovely ground-trailing tresses than he is in protecting his charges. But when he cries "wolf" twice, a determined fairy decides to teach him a lesson once and for all.

BOOK 2: UNSOILED

When Elle finds herself practically enslaved by her stepmother, she scarcely has time to even clean the soot off her hands before she collapses in exhaustion. So when Thorny tries to convince her to go on a quest and leave her identity as Cinderbella behind her, she consents. Little does she know that she will face challenges such as a determined huntsman, hungry dwarves, and powerful curses . . . .

BOOK 3: ROSEBLOOD

Both Elle and Thorny are unhappy with the way their lives are going, and the revelations they have had about each other have only served to drive them apart. What is a mother to do? Reunite them, of course. Unfortunately, things are not quite so simple when a magical lettuce called "rapunzel" is involved.

If you're a fan of thieves with a heart of gold, then you don't want to Miss . . .

THE PRINCES AND THE PEAS
A TALE OF ROBIN HOOD

A NOVEL OF THIEVES, ROYALTY, AND IRREPRESSIBLE LEGUMES

BY LELIA EYE

An infamous thief faces his greatest challenge yet when he is pitted against forty-nine princes and the queen of a kingdom with an unnatural obsession with legumes. Sleeping on top of a pea hidden beneath a pile of mattresses? Easy. Faking a singing contest? He could do that in his sleep. But stealing something precious out from under "Old Maid" Marian's nose . . . now that is a challenge that even the great Robin Hood might not be able to surmount.

When Robin Hood comes up with a scheme that involves disguising himself as a prince and participating in a series of contests for a queen's hand, his Merry Men provide him their support. Unfortunately, however, Prince John attends the contests with the Sheriff of Nottingham in tow, and as all of the Merry Men know, Robin Hood's pride will never let him remain inconspicuous. From sneaking peas onto his neighbors' plates to tweaking the noses of prideful men like the queen's chamberlain, Robin Hood is certain to make an impression on everyone attending the contests. But whether he can escape from the kingdom of Clorinda with his prize in hand before his true identity comes to light is another matter entirely.

About the Author

Jann Rowland is a Canadian, born and bred. Other than a two-year span in which he lived in Japan, he has been a resident of the Great White North his entire life, though he professes to still hate the winters.

Though Jann did not start writing until his mid-twenties, writing has grown from a hobby to an all-consuming passion. His interests as a child were almost exclusively centered on the exotic fantasy worlds of Tolkien and Eddings, among a host of others. As an adult, his interests have grown to include historical fiction and romance, with a particular focus on the works of Jane Austen.

When Jann is not writing, he enjoys rooting for his favorite sports teams. He is also a master musician (in his own mind) who enjoys playing piano and singing as well as moonlighting as the choir director in his church's congregation.

Jann lives in Alberta with his wife of more than twenty years, two grown sons, and one young daughter. He is convinced that whatever hair he has left will be entirely gone by the time his little girl hits her teenage years. Sadly, though he has told his daughter repeatedly that she is not allowed to grow up, she continues to ignore him.

Website: http://onegoodsonnet.com/
Facebook: https://facebook.com/OneGoodSonnetPublishing/
Twitter: @OneGoodSonnet
Mailing List: http://eepurl.com/bol2p9

Made in United States
North Haven, CT
23 September 2022